P9-DDZ-217

CHILD

of the

DAWN

CHILD

of the

DAWN

A Magical Journey
of Awakening

GAUTAMA CHOPRA

FOREWORD BY DEEPAK CHOPRA

AMBER-ALLEN PUBLISHING ◆ SAN RAFAEL, CALIFORNIA

© 1996 Gautama Chopra

Amber-Allen Publishing, Inc.
Post Office Box 6657
San Rafael, California 94903

Editorial and production: Janet Mills
Cover design: Nita Ybarra Design
Cover art: Scala/Art Resource, NY. Episode of the Bhagavata Purana.
   Guler Style, 18th century. National Museum, New Delhi, India.
Author photo: Deepak Singh
Typography: Rick Gordon, Emerald Valley Graphics
Printed by: R. R. Donnelley & Sons

All rights reserved. This book may not be reproduced in whole or in part, or transmitted in any form or by any means, electronic, mechanical, photocopying, recording, or other, without written permission from the publisher, except by a reviewer who may quote brief passages in a review.

Library of Congress Cataloging-in-Publication Data

Chopra, Gautama, 1975–
    Child of the dawn : a magical journey of awakening / Gautama Chopra.
        p. cm.
    ISBN 1-878424-24-6 (cloth)
    I. Title.
    PS3553.H588C48   1996   96-24527
    813'.54 — dc20   CIP

ISBN 1-878424-24-6
Printed in the U.S.A. on acid-free paper
Distributed by Publishers Group West

10   9   8   7   6   5   4   3   2   1

To my four grandparents:

Nani, Nana, Ma, and Daddy, who are the best examples of enlightenment, ageless wisdom, and innocence that I have ever known.

The same sun is newly born in new lands
in a ring of endless dawns.

– Rabindranath Tagore

CONTENTS

CONTENTS

Foreword
by Deepak Chopra

In the Vedic tradition of India there is a belief that one's name and form are inseparable. "Gautama" is an old name that literally means "the enlightened one." It was given to the ancient prince who attained enlightenment ages ago as the Buddha.

Gautama Chopra, my son, is a child of the dawn — the dawn of a new consciousness which is ready to transform the world. A critical mass of enlightened new leaders in the coming generation is necessary to ensure that our relationship to our Mother Earth once again becomes sacred and pure. I believe Gautama is one of these new leaders.

When Gautama was about four years old, my wife, Rita, and I made sure that he learned to meditate. Meditation was an important part of his upbringing, and he became familiar with the experience of inner silence at a very early age. He was also told that, although we had begotten him, he did not belong to us. He was a gift from the universe, and we were his caretakers for the time being. It has been our privilege and honor to have that role.

In *The Seven Spiritual Laws of Success*, I have written about "The Law of Dharma," which says that we are here for a purpose and that each of us has a unique gift or special talent to give to others. In accordance with this principle, Gautama was never told that he needed to perform well in school, get good grades, or go to the best colleges. He was only told that he must find out what his unique talents are and put them to the service of humanity. Today, Gautama is a young man of twenty-one years, a student at Columbia University with a passion for religious studies and literature. This book is an expression of his unique talents.

Child of the Dawn is a bold and provocative statement of freedom. It is about escaping the prison of the known and stepping into the unknown — the field of infinite possibilities. It is a testimony to the way in which "The Seven Spiritual Laws" can actually be lived in the life of a young boy, Hakim. Through Hakim's trials, tribulations, and adventures, one can glimpse how these principles can be a guiding light in our own search for meaning and empowerment.

Most of my books have been works of nonfiction. It is therefore liberating to see my son express the principles from *The Seven Spiritual Laws of Success* in a parable. Fiction in many ways expresses the truth more lucidly than nonfiction. As Tagore once said, "Truth in her dress finds facts too tight. In fiction, she moves with ease." When we discover the essential message of Gautama's book, we catch a glimpse of a reality that transcends the practical and touches upon the magical and the divine.

On our many travels to India, Gautama has witnessed the harsh reality of the street children who have no belongings other than their beautiful souls. In India, even amidst the immense poverty and destitute conditions, one finds in the children no trace of violence, no hostility, no rage, no anger. There is a simple, sweet innocence even among the extremely impoverished.

Child of the Dawn is a touching story about a child who is lost, alone, and seeking to find his purpose in life. This child exists within all of us. *Child of the Dawn* is a metaphor, in a sense, for all our lives. We come alone into this world, and one day we shall leave it all alone. In between, we meet as travelers for a few precious moments on a cosmic journey.

When Gautama was six years old we spoke about this. He said, "We came here on different trains, and we have encountered each other at the train station. Before we embark on separate trains again, on separate journeys, let's have fun!" He also told me that we had met before, a long time ago on a bridge near a mountain in Tibet and that we were in the habit of switching roles. We are all ancient souls, and indeed it is our destiny to play an infinity of roles. But we are not the roles we are playing. The alert witnessing of the roles we play is the first step on our journey of awakening.

I hope you will enjoy Gautama's book. If you are young, perhaps you will resonate with the dreams and aspirations of the principal character in this book. As you do so, you may find in his journey of awakening the story of your own life. And if you are not so young and are a parent like me, perhaps you will recognize, as I am beginning to, that our children are our greatest teachers.

It has been said that the child is father of the man. As I read the pages of this book, I am more convinced than ever that this, indeed, is true.

ACKNOWLEDGMENTS

THIS BOOK WOULD NOT HAVE BEEN POSSIBLE IF NOT for the efforts and attention of many people. I would like to express my love and gratitude in particular to:

Janet Mills, without whose loyalty, dedication, and professional skills as an editor, this book would have never emerged in its final form. Thank you, Janet. I love you!

Lynn Franklin for all your insight and guidance.

Arielle Ford for all your enthusiasm, love, and unsurpassed energy.

Peter Guzzardi for sharing your brilliance and wisdom and helping me to grow as a writer.

Uma Ergil for your countless hours spent silently behind the scenes.

Mom and Papa for giving me infinite possibilities through your unrelenting love and wisdom.

Mal for showing me, through your own example, the courage to pursue my dreams. What a year! Good luck. And even more so to you, Sumant.

All my family for all your unconditional love and support.

Candice for showing me what true beauty and friendship really are.

And last, but not least, my BOYZ (you know who you are) for making life laughs and fun. What's up?

LOST

HE WAS LOST. SOMEHOW DURING HIS YOUNG LIFE, HE had lost his way. Lost from where? Lost from what? Ah, well, you will see, we are not speaking of being lost in a labyrinth of streets in a twisted medieval city. His displacement, his disorientation, was of a more desperate and desolate nature, for he did not understand what he was lost from.

The child was alone, truly alone, with no mother or father, no family, no home — nothing to call his own. Each day, as dawn woke the sleeping metropolis, he watched the world pass him by. There was little reason to persevere. He had no one to love, no one to laugh with, no one with whom to share his deepest secrets. There were no enchanted memories, nothing sacred at all to hold close to his heart.

And then one day, inspired by his dreams of mirth and magic, he was drawn toward a search for power and lasting happiness. It was a search for meaning, a quest for love, the justification of his entire existence. And thus began his journey of awakening — a journey which led him from the realm of his dreams to a world of chaos, and back once more to a place where dreams really do come true.

1

ORPHAN OF THE CITY

HAKIM AWOKE WITH HIS ARMS OUTSTRETCHED AS IF to embrace the heavens, but he only caught the dirt kicked up from an antiquated car that rushed past his hideaway.

Dawn brought the familiar sounds of a crying baby seeking its mother's breast, the rooster's call, the whimpering of dogs, morning prayers and salutations, and the jingle of women's anklets and bracelets. Lingering smells of ash from burnt garbage mingled with incense to tantalize the air that slowly drifted by and drew him from another night's fantasies. Reluctantly, the child abandoned the world of his dreams for the prospects of a new day.

The world of the street orphan greeted Hakim as he opened his eyes. The city came to life as its characters donned their costumes and began to play their roles. Children headed for abandoned lots, picking up sticks and stones to serve as bats and balls for their games. Women started morning fires while their daughters washed clothes, thrashing them on rocks to drain the water from their broken threads. Men set off to thrift shops and stalls in the bazaar, anticipating a day of dozing and gambling, as elders chanted prayers to faceless Gods and Goddesses to protect and feed their families.

The sun's rays emerged from the paling darkness to paint the sky in brilliant shades of red, yellow, and blue. Slowly the heat crept into the shadows to scorch the streets of a fevered and bustling metropolis.

Each morning before the sun became too strong,

Hakim walked to a nearby intersection where he could wash windows and sell outdated magazines and bruised fruit stolen from the market the night before. There were few regular customers in the cars that passed. The faces always changed, but to Hakim they all possessed a similar identity: these were people who had lives — they had friends and family, they had money, they had power.

Hakim watched impeccably clad youngsters from the wealthy neighborhoods to the east make their way to the city's finest Catholic institution, a red brick building at one end of the street. Sometimes he would follow them to the looming walls that separated the school from the rest of the city. He would peer through the gates as the children drifted into a cross-topped chapel. Hakim always wondered what secret rituals drew hundreds of youngsters inside.

In the fields around the buildings, children played football and cricket, laughing and fighting with one another in their button-down shirts and knickers. Unlike children in the nearby villages, they had polished bats and balls, protective gear, and shining uniforms to use for recreation. In the evening Hakim imagined that they returned to lavish homes and beaming parents, emptying their swollen bags full of books, papers, and pencils. Their hearts held hopes and dreams of the future — hopes and dreams Hakim had never known.

From the west came a stream of tourists from the city's five-star intercontinental hotel. Hakim often wondered about the foreigners who crossed the seas to India to live in luxury. Sometimes he would dream that he was born to one of them and that someday he would reclaim his rightful place. He admired their wealth and opulence, their starched clothing and leather bags. Most of the hotel guests sat in polished air-conditioned cars to avoid exposure to the outside world. As traffic clustered by the hotel's gates, exhaust from the cars covered Hakim's olive skin with a thin layer of soot.

Hakim had run away from the city orphanage at the age of twelve. He had entered the streets brimming with confidence and dreams that had made his head spin. Unlike most street orphans, Hakim did not conspire with others, or join a beggars' group. By developing street smarts and savvy, he carved a place for himself and minded his own business. When Hakim fared especially well, he would share his earnings with other street children, often saving them from beatings by ruthless gang leaders who were anxious for their dues.

The children looked up to Hakim, admiring his independence and bold nature. For a street orphan, he was considered a success. But this was hardly enough for Hakim. After two years on the streets he realized the prison-like walls of his childhood in the orphanage still loomed around him. Hakim longed to escape from poverty and oppression and live in the opulence and grandeur he saw passing him on the street each day. With all his spirit, Hakim longed for that one thing he believed would bring him freedom and lasting contentment. That one thing was wealth. And he was willing to try anything, do anything, or go anywhere to attain it.

2

FORBIDDEN FRUIT

HAKIM EMERGED FROM THE CLOUDS OF DUST AND heat into the marketplace. His heart surged as if to match the pulse of the thriving market which spread life into every corner of the street. Fruits and vegetables of every kind and color spilled over the stalls as customers filled their baskets and haggled over prices. Smells of cinnamon, cumin, coriander, pepper, and mustard seed mingled with cow dung and the ever-pervasive dust to create an aura unique to the awakening bazaar.

Hollow voices carved the sweaty air as merchants cried out the names of their products and sang their prices, hoping for abundant sales. Their cries echoed off the dusty stone walls that surrounded the ancient market. Wandering cows wove between meandering people, while stray dogs sniffed every piece of filth in search of a morsel to eat.

A cloud of dust cast a yellow haze over the entire scene. Sunlight filtered through the haze, throwing shadows from the stone walls onto the hardened earth. These same shadows had been there for centuries, reappearing at the same time each day for countless ages. The actors had changed through endless generations, but the script and stage had stayed the same.

Every morning shopkeepers unpacked their wares, then sat with crossed legs in front of their makeshift stores to market their products: foreign fabrics, exotic foods, rich oils, opulent jewels, and the ambitious promises of healing elixirs.

Quietly Hakim observed the morning's activities: the secret rendezvous, the shadowy deals and daily dramas that people took so seriously. Cultured house-wives shopped on their way home from morning coffee and manicures; scholars rummaged through ancient books to find stained pages of Chaucer and Yeats. Retired businessmen sat in handy-shops, searching through mountains of metal for a particular screw to fit a radio they had bought forty years before.

A strong hunger rumbled in Hakim's stomach, one that could not be alleviated by the scanty morsels of food that lay in his hideaway under the bridge. In one glimpse, he assessed his opportunities to obtain some food. Juicy mangoes and melons gleamed in the sunlight, making Hakim salivate as he decided which stall to target.

At the far end of one alley, Hakim noticed a young woman dressed in a fiery orange sari, uncovering her stand to reveal brilliant yellow and green mangoes. A black cow roamed lethargically past one side of the stall, sweeping the ground with his snout in search of food. Hakim glided swiftly and silently behind the massive animal. Crouching behind the animal's flank, he watched the woman carefully unpack her goods from her cart. Her face was delicate and neither smiling nor sad. She was fully focused on the task in front of her.

Hakim peered beneath the veil that shielded her forehead, at her tender brown eyes. They were soft and gentle and seemed to tell a story all their own. Deep down, he knew she would understand him, empathize with him, even wish to help him relieve his hunger. Silently he thanked her before coyly approaching the stall to make his catch.

From the corner of her eye, Sunali spied a small arm cloaked in brown linen emerge from behind a standing cow and reach into her stall. Instead of seizing the arm or striking it, Sunali choked back a smile as she saw the little hand hover over one piece of fruit and then another, finally settling for the biggest of the lot.

With more than a bit of compassion, Sunali carried on, pretending not to see the theft as it unfolded. She took an extra moment to rummage through an empty sack by her feet, not wanting to disturb the street orphan's venture and bruise his pride.

"Trying to steal a mango, are we?" The thunderous voice assaulted Hakim just as he felt a heavy knee crash into his side, forcing him to drop the prized fruit. The cow, disturbed from its slumber, cried out a low rumbling moo and kicked up dirt into Hakim's face. "These are obviously not the manners I taught you."

After reorienting himself for a moment, Hakim gazed up at the face of his one-time orphanage headmaster. The Master's features were dark and refined. Thin eyebrows sat below a broad forehead, framing his dark eyes. His hair was long, black, and thick; a finely manicured beard gave an imperious look to his sharp chin. He was tall and slim, and he wore a long dark cloak that accentuated his forbidding appearance.

Hakim looked up at the man, recalling all the contempt and fear he had felt for him. He noticed again, as he always did, the large mole that protruded near the Master's right eye. It was the lone imperfection on his otherwise sharp and handsome face.

Hakim recalled all his years in the orphanage where this portentous man was in charge. Along with the other orphans, he had endured a near decade of abuse, an unending torrent of belittling remarks and crushing blows that held the children fearfully captive. Worst of all their tormentors was this man known only as the "Master."

The Master's interaction with the orphans was a game to him — a game the children had no chance of winning. Whatever money he garnered from corrupt government officials for the orphanage, he spent on his own desires. It was a well-kept secret that he put the orphans to work for him and barely fed them for their efforts. So while the Master had anything and everything he ever wanted, "his kids," as he liked to call them, struggled to survive.

Even now the Master seemed indifferent to the fate of one of his runaways. He had knocked Hakim down on his knees and was clutching the boy's collar with his long, lean hand. The Master smiled into

Sunali's startled eyes after crudely studying her hand some figure from head to toe.

"I assure you, madam, this is not the type of behavior I teach my boys. This one" — he flicked Hakim's head with the back of his hand — "got away from us before we knocked any sense into him."

The Master carried himself as royally as a king. He knew how to command the attention of an audience, and he was equally adept in charming a woman. But he had frightened Sunali with his sudden forcefulness. "I can only teach those who are willing to learn," he said, raising his eyebrows and looking intently at the young woman.

Sunali looked troubled and helpless. With a surge of chivalry, Hakim struggled to free himself from the Master's grasp, but found himself quite helpless. The Master turned his head to fix his eyes on Hakim. In an ominous voice he uttered, "Never treat a woman with such disrespect that you steal from her."

The young boy shuddered for a moment in the grasp of his Master, as the object of his intensifi

stare. Under his breath the Master whispered to Hakim, "Forbidden fruit should only be tasted by those who can take it without getting caught. Let that be a lesson to you, son — from your Master." He tightened his grip on Hakim's neck as Sunali gasped.

"Pick it up," the Master ordered in a stern voice, nodding at the bruised fruit lying on the ground. "Pick it up and give it to the woman." Again, he jabbed Hakim hard with his knee, making him crouch over a second time. Rage boiled in Hakim's stomach as he looked up at the man's sharp features and drew in the ugly mole. A slight smile surfaced on the Master's face, as if he were proud to inspire such a response.

Hakim turned to grab the fruit and discovered Sunali's hand reaching toward it. He locked eyes with hers, which were now filled with tears. "Please, madam, allow me." Hakim's frown turned into a mischievous and cunning grin. He reached out and grabbed the oversized mango that squeezed in his hand, emitting little streams of juice. Clenching it

tightly, in a sudden blur of movement he swung his arm around and crushed it into the Master's groin. The Master, seized with pain, folded over and bellowed out a high-pitched cry of distress. Caged chickens in the neighboring butcher shop squawked wildly in response to the outburst. Hakim raised himself up from his knees and turned to Sunali.

"Madam, I apologize . . . "

"Run!" she screamed, and with surprising swiftness reached out and pulled him away from the attempted grasp of the Master.

Hakim turned to Sunali and humbled by her silent laughter, returned a bashful grin. Then he smiled triumphantly at the Master, who was still hunched over in a cramp. Modestly he clasped his hands together and saluted Sunali goodbye before quickly disappearing into the crowd.

Hakim was adept at losing himself in the twisted streets of the marketplace. He did not wander far, knowing there was little possibility that the Master could catch him. Hidden to the side of an ice-cream stall, Hakim watched the Master stumble away like a drunken sailor as Sunali hurriedly pushed her cart in the opposite direction.

With glassy eyes, the Master searched the crowd for any trace of Hakim, but he did not chase after the boy. Instead of frowning at his apparent humiliation, a self-satisfied smile spread across his face. The Master knew he could not catch the fleet-footed child, but deep in his soul he also knew their paths would cross again.

3

THE MASTER'S CHAMBER

Hakim moved rapidly through the winding streets and crowded markets thinking of ways to strike back at the Master. The hunger in his stomach was almost forgotten as a deep-seated resentment took its place. Hakim was not sure why the Master could still evoke such strong feelings within him. His hatred for the Master was the strongest feeling he had ever known. And yet he admired the Master, secretly wishing that he, too, could one day command as much power and authority.

Hakim was determined to seek revenge for the humiliation he had suffered once again. He would teach the Master a lesson this time by stealing one of his priceless treasures. It didn't take him long to arrive at the top floor of the Master's chamber. Far removed from the rest of the decrepit orphanage, the Master's chamber and opulent dining quarters were locked away and hidden from the eyes of its frequent visitors.

Toward the end of his time at the orphanage, Hakim had discovered these hidden quarters and had learned how to sneak into them. Countless times he had ventured into this same forbidden place. He knew every floorboard in the balcony and how to avoid every squeak. Now he sat on the balcony curled behind a pillar, invisible to the men downstairs.

There was little conversation — at least none Hakim could hear. The Master reclined in his chair. He looked pensive, embroiled in his own foul mood, silently watching his son, Karun, feast on the lavish dinner set before him.

Karun, who was slimmer than his father, but greedier in his appetite, ate feverishly. Finally, having watched the boy devour an entire chicken then reach for another, the Master bellowed out, "We are finished. Take this away." Servants appeared in the doorway and approached the table. Karun's face darkened with displeasure.

"Father, I'm not done with the chicken," he said. He turned to address the servants. "Leave the . . ."

"Silence. You are done," his father interrupted. "Take it away, Shanti," he ordered the hesitant servant.

Karun, frustrated, squinted his narrow eyes and shot a threatening glance at the departing servant. His chin dripped with juices and food.

The Master looked at his son with disgust. He had given Karun every luxury, he had tutored him with the most renowned professors, yet the boy did not understand the fundamental lessons his father sought to teach him. Karun lounged around day after day, gambling with his friends, taunting the orphans, and bullying the helpless servants.

The boy turned his attention to his father, who had now shut his eyes as if it would aid his digestion. "Father, some city officials dropped by again complaining about this and that — the overcrowding, the lack of space, the shortage of food." His voice filled with arrogance. "But I took care of it."

The Master opened his eyes and peered at the boy, who continued smugly. "I sent them on their way with a little gift, and everything was okay." The boy paused for a moment. "Father, I had them eating out of my hands."

"Did you?" the Master replied.

"It's become somewhat of a bore, you know. Honestly, Father, I intimidate those worthless bureaucrats, as well as the little rats in this place. They all jump to attention whenever I enter the room. I find it rather amusing to command that kind of power." He smiled, arrogant and triumphant.

The Master's eyes were still closed. "You call that *power*, son? You call throwing money at ignorant bureaucrats — you call intimidating orphans and

worthless street rats *power*? You are a real fool, Karun."
He opened his eyes and leered at the boy.

Karun, deflated, looked at his father. "What do
you mean?"

"What I mean," the Master replied, "is that you
don't know the first thing about power."

"Father, I don't have time for your philosophy,"
Karun said, in an effort to regain his pride.

"What do you mean you don't have time, you
silly idiot? I have tried to put you in charge of this
place, but you can't look after it. I saw one of your
'little rats' scampering in the market today. I caught
him stealing when he should be back at the orphanage, working for us." Hakim felt anger boil up in his
chest at the mention of the morning's encounter.

"Karun, you don't have the ability or the authority to manage this place. Perhaps it's time you
earned it."

"But it's mine already, Father," the boy declared.

"This is yours?" the father said, exasperated. "You
actually believe this is yours?" He lashed out with his

forearm at a goblet in front of his son, flinging wine all over the boy's chest, staining his white shirt.

The boy, staring angrily at his father, attempted a response. "What . . ."

"This is mine, Karun. All this is mine, and even if I choose to give anything to you," — he paused and raised his voice — "it still shall not be truly yours until you have earned it!" His fury was rising.

Hakim smiled at the Master's rage. Karun had always disgusted him. He had boldly paraded around the orphanage, issuing demands to everyone in sight, hiding behind hired thugs to ensure that people heeded his every desire. No one respected him, but they obeyed his commands because they feared the power of his father.

Karun was somewhat confused. He shifted in his chair uneasily, leaning back with an air of defiance.

The Master looked at his son incredulously. Seeing the pathetic prospect before him intensified his rage. He rose from his chair and thrust the table over, spilling the remaining cups and plates onto the floor.

Karun, stunned, stumbled from his chair. The Master stormed back and forth across the room.

"What I have tried to teach you, Karun, what you seem incapable of grasping, is that power comes from within. The title you enjoy, the position you attain, is not the basis of true power. These could come or go at any time. And then you'll have nothing."

The Master looked directly at his son, "What would you do if I took away your money or took away your position? What power would you have then? Who would listen to you, Karun? The power you enjoy depends on other people to sustain it. That is not true power.

"True power comes from knowing what you want and from taking action to get it. It comes from the *self* — the *inner* self, not your inflated ego, Karun. When you understand how to harness that power, everything and more will come with that understanding."

The Master's voice turned quiet. Hakim leaned in closer to hear the Master's words. "I am telling you this for your own benefit, for *our* benefit, Karun. The things we might do together. . . . Think of the *true* power you would have to control your destiny and create all the wealth you could ever desire!"

"Father, if you have this knowledge you speak of already," — Karun's eyes lit up again, having recovered from his fear — "then share it with me."

"Indeed I have it, but I have it myself. These are things you must learn on your own, through your own efforts. No one can give you the desire to succeed — that must come from you. Without desire, there is no action; without action, there can be no results. Desire is one of the keys to wealth and power. Unfortunately, your every need is indulged. You have no desire to do anything, Karun." The Master paused as if realizing the futility of his explanations.

"Father," the boy started.

"Be silent, Karun, and you might even learn something. I used to be like you, obsessed with a life of drinking and gambling, obsessed with power — or what I believed was power — giving orders and having servants fulfill my every wish." The Master closed his eyes for a moment, remembering lost days.

"But I was fortunate. At an early age I learned the principles that enable me to generate wealth, command the respect of others, and control my own destiny. I learned these secrets by . . ." He hesitated for a moment.

"By what?" Karun interjected.

The Master tilted his head as if to retrieve the thought from his memory. "I met someone," he said in a peculiar tone. "I found this old man, known as the 'wise one,' who lives in one of the villages. . . ."

"But Father," Karun interjected, "you have brought me to these gurus and teachers since I was a child. I have already learned the sciences and scriptures from them. Which wise one do you speak of?"

The Master responded with obvious frustration. "Karun, you must find him yourself. The wise one can only be found by you. It is your own desire that will attract his wisdom to you.

"It was the wise one who taught me the secrets of true power. You must find the wise one yourself,

Karun. Each of us must do this for ourselves. A wealth of knowledge more precious than any gold awaits you when you do."

Hakim leaned over the banister, his curiosity mounting.

The Master was now almost whispering as he spoke to his son. "You see, your thoughts and feelings have magnetic power. They are the magnet that draws people, circumstances, and events to you. Whatever you put your attention on increases in your life. Everything you ask for comes easily when you understand the source of your power and know how to put it to use."

He stared at his son for a moment. "You'd like to command *that* kind of power, wouldn't you?"

Hakim felt tremendous excitement at the idea of such awesome power. This was the key to the wealth he longed for. The Master walked toward the door, preparing to leave the room.

"Father, where do I find this fellow?" Karun asked skeptically. He paused and took a deep breath, "The 'wise one,' as you call him. Why can't you simply tell me what you have learned from him?"

The Master turned to face his son. The whining tone of distrust in the boy's voice did not escape his notice. It was useless to teach this boy anything. "I don't know, Karun, but I hear the carnival is in town. Perhaps you should start there."

The Master grunted and turned once again toward the door. Hakim suddenly realized that he was not concealed anymore, but almost perilously hanging over the balcony. He pulled back, but he had moved too quickly. The shift in his weight caused the floor to creak. He held his breath, closed his eyes, and prayed with all his might. Tears filled his eyes at the thought of being captured and returned to the orphanage.

Karun had not noticed a thing, but the Master had stopped in his tracks. He could sense the presence of someone in the shadows. Looking up at the balcony, he saw nothing. The Master lowered his head and continued out the door, mumbling some words to himself.

The Master had been too engrossed in conversation with his son to notice the disturbance on the balcony. Now that he was aware of another presence, he could feel the curiosity looming in the air, a passionate desire ignited by his speech. He knew it wasn't his son who would find the secrets of the wise one. There was another boy with potential. It had been a long time since he felt an energy that strong, a curiosity so penetrating. It reminded him of his own strong will and determination.

The Master had often wondered who besides his son might claim the wisdom he embodied and help him to extend his domain of influence. Even the most selfish of men, as the Master truly was, might want to share the secrets of his success with one who could carry on his legacy. He had yearned to be the mentor for such a student. And now he felt it creeping into his own house, coming to him and beckoning him for counsel. "Ah yes," he said to himself. "Perhaps another student. This one has it in him."

4

SHADOWS OF THE NIGHT

OVERWHELMED BY HIS DESIRE TO FIND THE WISE ONE
and his secrets to power, Hakim walked swiftly down
the road leading away from the orphanage. He knew
the Master's words could lead the way to his destiny.
But now he was tired and worn out from the day's
events. Hakim had little energy to spend trying to
fully understand what he had overheard.

With one last glance at the children in captivity,
Hakim slipped out of the orphanage and wandered

through the crammed streets toward his hideaway under the bridge. Barely ten minutes after walking the city streets, he noticed a young boy on the side of the road. He was an orphan like Hakim. The boy was small-framed and thin, certainly no older than Hakim, and his face expressed a mix of sadness and desperation. It was an expression Hakim was accustomed to seeing in street orphans.

Tears welled up in the child's eyes, tears full of loneliness and despair. Hakim knew that feeling; he had felt his own tears swelling up inside him, rising from deep within his soul. Hakim had avoided the danger of succumbing to his sorrow. Now this boy would have to do the same.

Hakim continued to study the boy from across the street. This boy looked new to the streets, and partly for that reason, Hakim's heart went out to him. The frightened, lonely look on the boy's face made Hakim want to reach out to help him. But the gnawing hunger in his own stomach reminded Hakim that he had nothing to offer. He turned away, leaving the boy behind.

Dusk had set in as Hakim continued to wind his way past stalls and stores, past cars and bicycles. Finally, he reached the cool shadows beneath the bridge, and slipped into his collection of blankets and shawls that served as a bed. A wave of sleepiness washed over him. The world spiraled away in a funnel of exhaustion, and his body gave in to slumber.

Minutes passed. The chaos of the daytime world subsided as he entered the world of his dreams. Another day had ended, and now Hakim could wear new masks for his night's adventures and escapades. Returning to the night, he could enter the worlds of kings and queens, of warriors and passionate lovers. He could rule lands and shape his own destiny, rewrite history and leave his legacy. In his dreams, he possessed everything he wanted. He was powerful and wealthy, handsome and respected — but most of all, he was loved. These illusions comforted and consoled him, because at least in his dreams he possessed the keys to wealth and happiness.

The smell of jasmine filled the air, and a nightingale

began to sing its song. Hakim lay curled in his lonely corner when a majestic presence appeared in the shadows. She wore a simple green shawl that covered her head and fell down to her ankles. Her face was thin and her features were delicate. She wore no makeup and not a piece of jewelry, with the exception of one brilliant green stone in a ring on the smallest finger of her right hand. Her presence brought light to the shadows around her, scattering the darkness like dust in the wind. Her movements were soft and silent as she glided toward the sleeping boy. On her head she balanced a woven basket.

She approached the boy with tenderness born of a desire to bless him and protect him from harm. She looked at Hakim with a sense of knowing, as if feeling something that neither he nor the world could yet feel. Tears of compassion filled her eyes but did not drop to the dusty ground.

She began to turn away, then paused and reached into her basket to recover a large green mango. She held it in her hand for a moment, then silently bent over and placed it by the sleeping boy. With one last glance at the small figure, she stepped out of the shadows of the bridge and disappeared into the crowded streets.

In the quiet hours before dawn, Hakim dreamed he was a king who lived in a heavenly palace beneath a bright blue sky. The elegant robes he wore, laced with gold-embroidered cloth, flowed behind him, dragging heavily across pristine marble floors. He emerged into a courtyard where thousands of bystanders hailed him and bowed in adoration. A multitude of servants swarmed around him, offering wines and meats. They waved fans to protect him from the heat, never allowing his skin to perspire.

He passed through the courtyard into a massive room of high ceilings and spectacular grandeur. Sprawling tapestries hung from royal oak walls. Suddenly he was sitting at the end of a long table, staring at a feast of roasted chickens. Dancers performed by his side, evoking the drunken laughter of numerous courtiers who suddenly appeared all around him.

On the wall to his left he noticed a long line of portraits. Kings crowned with gold peered down with stern faces. He searched the royalty stretching far down the wall until he saw a face that resembled his own. He inspected it closely. There he was: wrapped in royal robes, carrying a scepter studded with diamonds. As he gazed at the next canvas, a portrait suddenly emerged from its blank surface. It was another king dressed in royal finery. The laughter died and Hakim's admirers turned away from him, leaving him all alone.

Suddenly he found himself back in the courtyard amongst the crowds, dressed in his worn brown linen shirt. The new king emerged from the marble palace and stared into the crowd. No longer was Hakim the center of attention; no longer did he wear the regal symbols of power, the evidence of his wealth and importance. The blue skies instantly turned black, and he found himself completely alone.

Hakim awoke with a single thought: *I must find the wise one and his secrets to power.*

Simple enough. If he could find the wise one and learn his secrets, Hakim could have all the wealth and respect he ever wanted. So, too, might he find the happiness he longed for.

With all his heart, Hakim believed this wisdom should be his. He had suffered long enough in a loveless, lonely existence. It was as though a life had been lived through him, but hardly lived at all. Why shouldn't he have the kind of life the hotel guests enjoyed or the schoolchildren inherited from their wealthy families? Moreover, why should the Master have exclusive claim to the power he spoke of?

Then that was it. He would leave the city in search of the wise one. Hakim recalled the conversation between the Master and Karun. He pictured Karun's greedy smile and the sparkle in his eyes when his father spoke of him having true power. Hakim hated to think there were seeds of the same greed sprouting in the depths of his soul. But even if there were, he would never be as mean or as selfish as Karun. Once he learned the secrets to wealth and happiness, he would share his knowledge with other street orphans. He would have something of value to give to the others.

In that instant Hakim resolved to leave his hideaway under the bridge — the only place, for all its filth, that had ever felt like home. Far from the streets of this city was a wise one who could change his destiny.

5

MAGIC OF MIND

HAKIM FOUND HIMSELF WONDERING ABOUT THE carnival that had come to town. He had overheard the Master telling Karun to look for the wise one there. Surely the Master was joking. But it was also true that any member of the roving road show would have traveled through many towns and villages in India. Perhaps someone at the carnival *could* help him find the wise one.

Hakim traversed the crowded streets, weaving between scooters, cyclists, and pedestrians until finally a giant purple Ferris wheel appeared on the skyline. The sight of the Ferris wheel awakened the urge to play, but Hakim reminded himself of the importance of his task.

Painted trailers dotted the fairground that had once been a beach. Hearing the squeals and laughter of children, Hakim hurried toward a small gathering of people outside a giant yellow trailer. Peering inside, he saw a magician wearing a long blue robe embroidered with golden stars and half moons. Long white hair flowed out from his pointed hat, cascading over his shoulders. A long white beard gave his face an air of wisdom.

Silver stars and floral arrangements hung on the walls of the trailer. Black sheets covered the windows. Sitting on a stool, surrounded by paraphernalia, the magician was performing standard tricks: pulling rabbits from hats and finding coins behind children's ears.

The younger children laughed, but some of the older ones left upon seeing the routine tricks. The magician didn't seem to mind. A small boy moved in close, almost beside the magician, who reached beside the child's ear and came away with his hand wrapped in a fist. He opened it to reveal a silver coin. "Uh, uh, uh," he warned playfully. "Come too close, and I'll have to charge you extra."

The children giggled at the magic. The magician reached beneath his stool and pulled out a colorful ceramic mask. It was half white and half black with silver-lined holes cut out for the eyes and painted red lips beneath the chiseled nose.

"One of many masks, many faces." The magician put the mask in front of his face, then tossed it aside and placed another and another in front of his face. "All different masks we wear, all different faces, but underneath we are the same being. Now that's real magic!" He grinned. The crowd shuffled, unimpressed. The magician, undisturbed by his audience's displeasure, smiled with affection as he fixed his eyes upon Hakim.

Then he spoke loudly to his young audience, abruptly ending his routine. "The sand feels nice between your toes. Children, take your parents to the beach. Don't forget to remove your shoes." He turned away and quickly began to pack his things as the crowd dispersed in confusion.

Hakim approached the magician.

"Excuse me, sir," Hakim said politely. "I was hoping you might tell me . . . Well, I'm looking for an old man known as the 'wise one.'"

"M'name's Maloney, and I'm from Wales. Not Irish, not Scottish, and definitely not British. I'm Welsh."

"Sir, I was thinking that maybe since you — "

Maloney cut him off. "Some say I'm a sandwich short of a picnic." He smiled. "Perhaps I am. Come with me, maybe we can find this person," — he paused and looked at Hakim with smiling eyes — "this wise one you are looking for."

Hakim followed the man through the crowds, until finally they reached a sprawling yellow tent. "This will serve well enough," Maloney muttered to himself. His expression was soft, but his eyes were bright, mirroring the orange and purple hue of the western sky.

Hakim followed Maloney into the tent, unwilling to abandon the man at this point. Inside, the tent was nearly dark. Dim lights lit their way until at last they came upon a wall of carnival mirrors.

"I wonder if you'd come here, son." Maloney motioned Hakim toward him and the mirrors. He stepped back to sit on a chair that appeared from nowhere. Hakim became conscious of the sudden silence that enveloped them. He listened carefully for carnival noises, but there was nothing. He looked around. It was dim, but he could make out a large open space. He wondered how they could still be inside the tent they had entered.

"You figured the space inside this tent was a certain size when we entered it." Maloney echoed Hakim's thoughts. "Space and time are illusions, my friend. The mind is a master magician. Loves to play tricks on us. Likes us to believe there's a limit to what we can dream, what we can do, I suppose. It's no wonder I have a job to do, reminding everyone about the real magic. . . . "

Maloney chuckled to himself and then continued. "There's nothing but pure potential all around us, son. Pure potential is the stuff we're made of. The mind is infinite, stretches farther than you can think. Not much to know once you realize this truth. It's all right there." He tapped his fingers on Hakim's chest and laughed. "Now, that's real magic, yes?"

Maloney pointed to Hakim's image in the mirror, a squat, plump version of Hakim, far removed from the scrawny figure he knew himself to be. It wasn't the first time Hakim had seen mirrors play tricks with his reflection. He had been to the carnival when he was very young, rushed from stall to stall, shuffled from tent to tent, and rushed back to the orphanage.

"Is this you? Is it the real you that you see?" Hakim turned and saw the white-bearded man giggling behind him. "Well, then." He cleared his throat and raised his eyebrows. "What about this one, son?"

Hakim gazed in the mirror. The image that stared back at him was now tall and skinny.

"Is that your *self* you see?" Maloney seemed intent on evoking an answer.

Hakim felt anxious. *Obviously not. These are games for children,* he thought to himself.

"Yes, yes — and now," the voice was relentless, forcing Hakim to look back in the mirror. "Is this your *self*?" A ripple of infectious laughter trailed his voice.

Hakim looked closely at the reflection in the mirror. Surely it was himself that he saw now. He scrutinized his mouth, his narrow nose. Suddenly he realized he was not so familiar with his own face.

"Indeed, you did come to this carnival years ago. I was in Wales at the time," the voice said reassuringly. "But I wonder if this is the same face you saw then. Or the same face you saw the very first time you looked in a mirror. Whose face is it you see in your dreams? Whose face will you wear when you are old and gray? The faces you wear are like characters in a play, but your *self* is the creator of all these characters."

The voice was soothing, as if it were touching a distant memory inside him, and Hakim felt calmed by it. "Beyond this world of illusion, there is a dreamer who manifests the dream. Don't ask who you see, because you will only see disguises. Ask who is doing the seeing.

"You are seeking someone you already know, my boy. You are looking outward when the one you seek is within."

There was silence. The seconds that followed seemed to stretch into hours. When Hakim looked up, the mirror had disappeared. Maloney was gone, and so was the chair in which he'd been sitting. Hakim looked around. The light was still dim, but the space was absolutely empty, as if nothing had ever been there. The sides of the tent blew gently in the breeze, kicking up dirt as they touched the ground.

Hakim hurried out of the tent. Maloney was leaning calmly against a food stall eating a sandwich.

6

SEEDS OF FORTUNE

JUST AS HAKIM WAS ABOUT TO ASK MALONEY WHAT
had happened, a throng of children ran up to the
magician and pleaded to see his tricks. Hakim was
contemplating his next move when he noticed an old
man with a small gathering of people around him.
Hakim moved closer to hear what the old man was
saying.

Could this be the wise one the Master spoke of? he
wondered. The old man was thin and haggard. His

body looked like a collapsible piece of furniture, neatly folded into a sitting position. His head was bald. The tattered clothing he wore was stained from dirt and wear.

The small brown varnished bowl that he held in his lap was empty now, and the old man was looking to fill it by telling a story. He coughed forcefully, then looked around at his audience, wanting to tailor his story just right. The old man fixed his eyes on Hakim as he began to speak.

"This is a story about two farmers from a very long time ago. The two farmers worked for Indra, the king of the heavens, and they understood it as their duty to produce crops and grains for his kingdom. The men felt very blessed to be employed directly by Indra, and they wanted to please him.

"One day Indra called the two men to his court and told them, 'In one year I am having a great assembly. Everyone will be there, and I will need to have the finest crops from both of you. I want you to concentrate on that one purpose for the next year.'

"Both of the men were grateful to be of service, and immediately returned to their farms to begin their work.

"Upon reaching his farm, the first farmer ripped out all the old crops and planted a thousand seeds. He yoked his bulls and watered his fields with a thousand buckets of water.

"The other farmer went back to his farm, planted a handful of seeds in the small plot of dirt outside his house, then watered the seeds while thanking the Gods for their growth.

"As the days passed, the first farmer began to worry about his plants. He tended his crops all day, driving his bulls over the field many times to give them extra water. He kept watching his crops, concerned about the fate of every seed. He thought, *How could I be so blessed by Indra? I must not fail him.* Even at night he would dream about his crops; he would dream about failure. His heart was overcome with fear, and when he woke up sweating in the middle of the night, he thought, *I shall not fear, I shall work harder.* But fear still lurked in his heart.

"The other farmer continued in his own manner of doing things. Each morning he stepped outside his doorway and poured a little water over the small plot of earth. People might think the fellow strange, but he spoke kindly to his seeds and even sang to them. In the evening, he would say good night to his garden with gratitude in his heart. At night he slept peacefully, content that his plants would surely flourish.

"Finally, after a year had passed, Indra called the two farmers to his court. The two men stood before him, and he addressed them both saying, 'My assembly is tomorrow, what have you prepared?'

"The first farmer began trembling, 'I have nothing, Your Highness.' He was nearly in tears and consumed with guilt and fear. 'I tried very hard. I did not leave my plants for one day, so I cannot understand why I failed to produce anything. Please forgive me,' he pleaded.

"Indra looked to the second farmer, 'And you?'

"'Spare my brother, Your Highness. I have plenty of crops. I will give half of mine to him so that we are both able to serve you in abundance.'

"Indra looked at the two men. 'I am curious as well as confused. How can there be so much difference in what my two best farmers have produced? How did each of you pursue your task?'

"The first farmer began to tell his story: 'The first day I plowed the fields, planted one thousand seeds, and watered them. Every day I watched over my fields, searching for signs of growth. I cannot say why, but they failed to grow.'

"Indra looked at the second farmer, who began to tell his story: 'The first day, I planted a handful of seeds. I cared for them the way I care for all my children —'

"Indra interrupted, 'How is that?'

"The farmer continued. 'I raised them with love and affection. I gave them the nutrients and food they needed, and then I left them alone.'

"The first farmer turned to the other. 'Why did you leave your garden alone?'

"The man turned to the first farmer. 'So that Mother Nature could do her part,' he said. 'Parents cannot be with their children or watch them every moment to ensure that they grow into adults. It is the nature of life to grow — to flourish and expand. It is the nature of plants to flourish if given the right conditions for their growth. I gave my plants what they needed, and trusted Mother Nature to do the rest. She will always support us when we have faith that she will.'

"'But I planted one thousand seeds, and you planted a handful. How can this be?' the first farmer said.

"Indra followed up. 'Were you not afraid that your small handful of seeds would not be enough?'

"'I have been a student of farming for very long now,' said the second farmer. 'My grandfather was a farmer, and my papa was one before me. I have learned that within each seed is the potential for infinite abundance. When one plant flourishes and produces fruit, its seeds give rise to more plants that bear fruit. Each plant has more seeds than are necessary to continue its kind, and in that way, it is infinitely abundant. When I planted my seeds, I expected to receive an abundance. I thanked them for sharing their abundance, knowing I was nurturing an infinite amount more.'

"'But when I saw that my plants were not growing, I became scared and tried even harder!' exclaimed the first farmer. 'Were you never afraid that your plants would not grow?'

"The second farmer responded, 'I knew that fear could not help my plants to grow. Fear only causes us to create what we fear. Knowing this, I chose to plant love in my heart and nurture it with gratitude. Love chases fear away, and gratitude keeps love alive. Where there is love, there is no room for fear. I cannot serve you well, Indra, if I am not a happy man.'

"The first farmer spoke again, 'Now I see that I have brought my fears upon me by giving them my attention.' He looked up at Indra. 'What is my punishment for failing you?'

"Indra looked down at the man. 'I think you have suffered enough, worrying this past year, fearing the days to come, and feeling guilt for the days gone by.

There is another seed here, a seed of opportunity to learn and do better in the future. You are both invited to join the assembly tomorrow.'"

The old storyteller stopped speaking. Some listeners had already dropped coins and small bills into his bowl; others did so now. They themselves were poor, but they understood the cycle of giving: when one gives, one engenders receiving.

Hakim dug into his pockets, knowing he had nothing to give to the old man. He thought about darting away, but he knew his guilt would follow him.

The old man turned to Hakim. "Come, sit."

Hakim glanced around to be certain the storyteller was talking to him. Most of the onlookers were already walking away. Maloney had disappeared as well, but Hakim was not concerned. Somehow he knew the magician would reappear when the time was right.

Hakim approached the old man and sat beside him. "You need not have money in order to give," the old man said.

Hakim looked intently at the man. "But I have nothing else to give you." Hakim thrust his hands deep into his pockets, hoping that something might appear in the bottom of them.

"Child," the old man responded, "do not search in your pockets for what you have to give. Search in your heart. There is a special gift that can only come from you. Just as I am here to tell my stories, you are here to share your special gift."

"I don't know what mine is," Hakim said sincerely.

"Then search in your heart, child, and if there is stillness, you are on your way and are most fortunate."

Hakim was intrigued by these last words. *On my way to what? To whom?* He began to think.

"Stillness is the womb of creation, child. It lies in the silent space between every action."

Hakim interrupted. "I do not understand. How can I create anything by being still?"

The old man responded, "When you are still, you can *feel* the sound of your own heart beating. Is that not so?"

Hakim nodded as the old man continued. "And if you remain still and cover your ears, you may even *hear* the sound of your own heart. But what is more important is to *listen* to its guidance. If we are always active, if we are always listening to the noise of the outside world, we forget that our heart will guide us if we only listen. We forget where the source of our creativity comes from — stillness."

Hakim was mesmerized by the storyteller's words. *He is very wise*, Hakim thought to himself.

"Stillness establishes a connection with our own heart, and each heart is connected to the heart of humanity, the universal wisdom. That is why I say you are fortunate if there is stillness in your heart. In stillness, you can listen to your heart, and when you listen, you will know what you are here to give."

Hakim nodded slowly. He did not fully understand the old man's words, but he could sense there was truth in what he said.

Maloney suddenly reappeared at Hakim's side. "Shall we be off? There is another show to see."

Hakim looked up at Maloney, then turned to thank the storyteller, but the old man was already merging into the carnival crowd. Hakim followed him with his eyes for a moment, then stood and followed Maloney.

As Hakim and Maloney walked through the carnival, the magician began to speak. "When we understand our place within nature's symphony, we can live in harmony with nature's song." He looked back at Hakim.

"There are an infinite number of forces at work — for and against us as well, I'm afraid. Only when we understand these forces can we control our fate." He grinned at Hakim. "Come, I'll show you."

7

DESTINY FORETOLD

THE YOUNG ASIAN WOMAN CAUGHT MALONEY'S wink when he entered her tent with Hakim. She was thin and pale. Hakim stared at her small hands resting on a table covered with a black cloth. A green stone sparkled on the smallest finger of her right hand. Her black eyes, shining underneath thin eyebrows, reflected the green glitter of the stone. Long black hair flowed onto her shoulders, spilling down her slender back. She acknowledged Maloney's wink with a quick twinkle of her own and a warm glance at the boy. Then she turned her attention to the young woman who sat across from her.

"My name is Lamia. I am not a psychic or a star reader. I only read the cards that you choose. I explain the non-material entities that rule the inner workings of the universe. The cards that you choose from the Tarot are guides to the hidden elements that shape the course of your life. They tell a story of obstacles to be overcome and lessons to be learned."

She waved her hands over the empty table cloth. When she brought them back, a deck of royal blue cards lay spread across the table. A quiet gasp emerged from the woman seated across from her. Hakim watched intently, enchanted by the mysterious woman.

"Choose your magic." Her voice was directed at the woman who sat across from her. "You control your choices, and thus control your fate. Take six cards from the pile."

The woman picked the first card from the middle of the pack with little hesitation, but became more hesitant with each successive choice. Lamia picked up the woman's cards and spread the top three in a row, then two under that, and a final one beneath them. She inspected them for a moment, then fixed her gaze on Hakim as if to suggest something with her eyes.

"What is it that you would like to know?" Lamia asked the woman across from her.

The woman answered in a hushed tone. "My husband is a farmer, I have three young ones, and we greatly need the crops this year to be prosperous. I have come from the country to find out if it shall be otherwise . . ."

Lamia whispered back, "Let me see." She looked at the top row: Hermit, Emperor, Devil. "The top row reveals the current state of affairs." She looked carefully at the first card.

Hakim stepped closer, listening closely, hoping the cards would hold some meaning for him as well. Maybe they would guide him on his journey to find the wise one.

"The Hermit means solitude from the activity of the material world, a period of silent reflection. If you do not find that which you seek within, then you will never find it without." Her face straightened as she continued. "The hermit is the silent seeker. In solitude, the hermit finds multitudes, an infinity. Be prudent. There are impediments, even enemies" — she looked at the woman — "perhaps other farmers. One must reassess what has been learned prior to a new beginning."

She squinted as she looked at the cards, then focused squarely at the woman across from her. "Perhaps your husband has already planted the seeds in order that they may flourish." The woman nodded in agreement. Lamia nodded also. "Then that is good."

Lamia looked at the second card: Emperor. "The path of worldly power requires discipline. If followed properly, discipline results in mastery of whatever skill you seek." She paused and looked again at the farmer's wife. "Your husband must be patient and disciplined in the practice of his farming if he wants to achieve success." The woman nodded her head in understanding.

Lamia read the third and final card in the top row: Devil. The woman across from her shuddered at the name. Hakim himself shuffled his feet nervously.

"The Devil represents the impulse to abandon our dreams and forget our true essence. Sometimes we exchange the mysterious and ambitious for the functional and pragmatic. That is the seduction of the Devil. The Devil tries to hold us back from the heights we are capable of reaching."

She looked back at the woman. "Perhaps your husband should aim for the most productive harvest he has ever achieved." The woman shot a guilty but humble smile back at Lamia.

"The second row of cards reveals what is coming." Lamia spoke softly. Hakim read them: Chariot and Sun.

"The Chariot indicates a journey. A journey will often bring one full circle, back to the beginning. But just because one ends where one begins does not imply lack of movement. The movement takes place within."

Lamia's voice took on a tone of concern. "The Chariot may test you by taking you through places of great confusion. Any major evolution captures the attention of evil. So beware." She looked at the farmer's wife. "Your husband may attract the attention of others in his quest for prosperity. Temptation lurks in every corner. Misuse of power is always seductive, but one must remain strong and determined. The right use of power brings you what you want." The farmer's wife smiled again.

Journey, prosperity, power, temptation — the words echoed in Hakim's head. He thought about his own journey before him, the search he had begun for the secrets to power. *Misuse of power is always seductive. . . .* Surely the Master had misused his power, but Hakim could not understand how he suffered because of it. Didn't the Master have all that he wanted?

Lamia's eyes met Hakim's, her voice reflecting her concern. "There are those who will attempt to sway your heart for selfish purposes, but remember, there is one who will always protect and guide you. One who will help you to make the right choices."

Lamia paused to let her words sink in before continuing. "The Sun card compliments your evolution. The Sun is about healing and light. The journey you are on is a journey of healing. Just as disciples go on a pilgrimage to seek their Gods, so, too, must the soul endeavor to find light. This is what the Sun card represents. Your husband's crops shall be very promising if they are carefully attended to. The Sun promises health and wealth on every level."

Lamia smiled slightly when she read the final card: Universe. "This is a very good card for you." The farmer's wife giggled modestly. "This is the fate you have chosen," Lamia said, peering at Hakim and Maloney from the side of her eyes. "The Universe card indicates the outcome of your journey — that all is at your disposal." She paused for a moment before continuing, "The Universe is union, the unity of individual and universal purpose. When the individual self is in alignment with the universal self, success is the natural outcome of every action. This means," — she turned to the farmer's wife — "very good crops."

The farmer's wife let out a gasp of relief, then quickly gathered her things as she struggled to get up from her chair. "Thank you . . . oh thank you. My husband shall be so pleased." She rushed from the tent. Lamia's eyes did not follow the woman, but rested instead on Hakim who stood by the doorway.

Hakim suddenly realized that he had been transfixed by the mysterious woman. Now with her gaze locked on his, he felt his face flush with heat.

"Come." Maloney's hand turned Hakim's shoulder, and he led him out of the tent. The carnival was dying down. The sky had turned blue-black, and the pounding of the waves grew louder as they walked toward the ocean.

"The crazy life of a Welsh carnival entertainer never ends. I move on tomorrow," Maloney said gently.

"What should I do now?" Hakim asked Maloney.

"Listen to your heart, and you will know what to do. What you do depends upon who you are." He smiled and pointed to Hakim's heart. "There is much wisdom in listening to your heart, and much joy in understanding your own identity.

"Be still, Hakim, and you will know that you are an instrument in the symphony of the universe. Enter into the harmony by finding the stillness inside, and you will feel nature's power move through you. It will always guide you."

Hakim turned to the water and gazed at the white foam of the waves crashing to the shore. When he looked back, Maloney was gone. Strangely, it didn't strike Hakim as all that odd. He was suddenly weary and could think only of finding a place to sleep. Hakim chose a large, dry rock, curled up on its smooth surface, and fell into a heavy slumber.

Lamia emerged from her tent and gazed at the stretch of beach where Hakim lay sleeping. There was affection and warmth in her eyes; in her hands she held six cards. She looked at them with a feeling of concern, then flipped one over — Chariot. She flipped another — Universe. The fortune-teller shot one final glance at the sleeping boy. Then she put the cards in her pocket and stepped back into her tent.

Silence infused the cool night air when suddenly the shadow of a figure appeared where Lamia had stood just moments before. A tall man emerged from the crowd of workers who were cleaning up and dismantling the carnival. He came out of the darkness as if he were made of it, with eyes that sparkled like jewels.

The Master smiled like a child in a candy shop. He had gone to sleep the previous night with renewed energy. The energy of excitement that had loomed in his dining hall had found its way to him. Upon waking, he had decided upon a jaunt to the carnival. Just as he had anticipated, a remarkable thing had happened: one of his kids, the insolent one in the market, had set out on a journey to find the secrets of the wise one.

The Master chuckled at Hakim's youthful inno-cence. But he was also impressed with Hakim's deter-mination to succeed. Hakim struck him as having real potential that only needed to be shaped and steered. The Master was increasingly excited by the idea that he might reel the young one in for his own purposes. He needed someone to collect his monies from the street people he employed — someone with street smarts, ambition, and desire.

Hakim would be lucky to have him as a mentor. What homeless child would not be enticed by the promise of luxury, prosperity, and power over others? Such temptation would taste sweet to one who had so little. Yes, he thought to himself, here was a chance to gain control of another young boy.

The Master stood nodding his head and feeling a smug sense of satisfaction in the choice he had made. He gazed through the dark to where Hakim lay curled up asleep. Slowly he moved in the direction of the rocks, leaving nothing but scattered sand as a trail.

8

OFFERING OF LOVE

HAKIM WOKE TO THE SOOTHING SOUND OF WAVES lapping against the shore. He looked across the beach to the carnival, where a few fixed buildings sat like silent, abandoned ruins of a lost city. Thin colored streamers and helium balloons waved in the breeze. The rest of the carnival had been broken down and packed away into trailers already moving off into the distance.

Hakim shifted his attention to the sky, where the transition from night to morning played out on the horizon. As if to adorn the world to which it would soon bring its warmth, the dawning light peeked over the horizon and colored the morning sky.

Hakim loved the dawn more than any other time of day. The moon, barely lucent, was sinking fast. Hakim could smell the sweet freshness of jasmine mixed with the salty ocean breeze. Aside from a few seagulls, Hakim was alone on the beach. But as he jumped off the rock he thought he heard a man's voice echo in his ears: *I'll be watching you.*

Hakim turned around quickly. No one was there. He felt a creepy sensation crawl across his skin. *That was odd*, he thought to himself. He looked around the beach again, then started toward the road.

Not far away, Hakim noticed footsteps leading to the ocean where a fisherman was standing by a pile of nets and buckets. As Hakim began to walk away, the man turned his head, revealing features as dark as the hair that fell from his hat. A black mole clung to the side of his face, but Hakim was moving too swiftly to notice. He scurried onto the road with its early morning traffic, grateful to be amidst people.

Weaving his way through the markets, Hakim stopped to snatch something to eat and satisfy his unending hunger. Not certain where to go next, he found himself drifting back toward familiar territory. He cut between narrow streets and back alleys behind the city's wealthy neighborhood. He looked up with envy at the houses he passed.

Lost in his thoughts, Hakim was roused by the smell of something burning. He raised his head and saw black smoke billowing up into the sky, so he scrambled through morning traffic to the gates leading into the cremation grounds. Hakim was always amazed at how his fear of death dissipated whenever he could profit from it. He had found that people became far more charitable when someone they loved had passed on. Whenever he noticed funeral processions or families gathered at the cremation grounds, he would put on a sorrowful face and invite the mourners' sympathy.

Hakim arrived just as the funeral pyre was engulfed in fire and smoke. Someone was overcome with grief, a scenario he had witnessed many times before. A small crowd was gathering around the fallen figure. He perched himself beneath a shady banyan tree, where he could watch without being noticed. Hakim was relieved to be back on familiar ground. Despite the fact that he had only been gone for one day, it seemed as though he had been on a long and wearisome journey.

Black smoke poured upward from the heap of wooden sticks. The fire crackled and hissed and spread until every branch was part of the roaring orange blur. A little girl stood near the fire, her neck stretched to watch the flames as they flickered upward. Dressed in white, she clutched her mother, who stood silently, tearfully beside her.

The fire reached a fierce climax and began to spit fiery gobs of sparks. Mother and daughter stepped back a couple of paces, the mother's eyes swollen with sadness. The little girl leaned forward as if to see if there might be some remnant of her father still inside it.

"Meena, be still!" Her overweight uncle pulled her back. "It's not time to play." The man's face was stern. He flashed a quick, authoritative eye at her, then straightened up to watch the flames.

Meena wondered why everyone was so sad. She looked around at the little circle that had gathered; each face had a solemn expression. Her aunts and uncles, even the holy man at the head of the fire, were silent with grief.

Meena wondered what had happened to Papa. She understood that something had changed, that her Papa was no longer with them. He was underneath the burning heap — that she understood. She knew Papa had been wrapped in a white cloth with flowers spread around him, and that his slumber was to be longer than the midday naps he took with her to avoid the heat.

She looked to her older sister. Devi would know what was going on. Meena had tried to whisper some words to her when they had marched in the procession earlier that morning. But her inquiries were met by stern orders to stay quiet. "I'll explain later, Meena. Stay silent . . . and cry!" her sister had ordered.

Meena was startled when all of a sudden her mother tightened her grip on Meena's small hand and emitted a piercing wail before her knees buckled. The little girl's aunts and uncles rushed forward to support her fallen mother. Meena's eyes were suddenly full of fear and sorrow.

"Meena, come here." Devi beckoned to her little sister. She grabbed Meena's hand and pulled her away.

The funeral pyre had finished burning; only sparks remained to dance on the charred sticks. A slender woman arrived, gripping a broom in her hand. She surveyed the scene for a moment before slowly sweeping the ashes at the base of the dying fire. She noticed two little girls out of the side of her eye. They were moving to the outskirts of the grounds, toward a small banyan tree. The branches of the tree gently rustled in the wind, providing a canopy of shade from the rising heat. At the base of the tree, a young boy sat silently — waiting.

Hakim watched as the two girls, dressed in white and holding hands, walked toward the tree where he was sitting. Often he had seen children coming here to say goodbye to their loved ones. Hakim envied them because he had never had the chance to say goodbye to his parents. He had never felt the loss of a loved one, nor had he ever been loved.

Hakim stared at the two girls, trying to figure out who they were, and how old. One was about his age, the other was younger, perhaps four or five years old. They paused when they noticed Hakim buried in the shadows of the tree. He caught himself, embarrassed to be staring at the older girl. She smiled and continued toward him, leading the younger one by the hand.

"Might we join you?" she asked. Hakim shuffled to one side so the two girls could sit beside him in the shade.

All three children sat quietly for some time, watching the family continue to comfort the stricken widow. The older girl lay a comforting hand on her sister's leg. Hakim lowered his head and stared at the ground. Not certain of what to say, he avoided the eyes of the older girl.

Finally, the younger girl broke the silence. "Where has Papa gone, Devi? What has happened to him?"

The older girl's stare was fixed on the dwindling fire. There was activity around her mother, but aside from that the only movement came from a lone woman sweeping ash in front of the pyre. Suddenly the woman turned as if to meet Devi's stare. At the same time, Hakim looked up and saw a flash of light come from the woman's hand. She was wearing some sort of green jewel that matched her clothing and sparkled brilliantly in the sunlight. Devi noticed it, too.

"Devi," the younger one said, pulling at her sister's arm, "what has happened to Papa?"

"Meena," she replied tenderly, "Papa used to have a life that allowed him to walk with us, but now he has a new life. It is different. He will no longer walk with us. That life has ended."

The younger girl tilted her head, showing her confusion. Hakim listened with interest. He, too, wondered what might have happened to his own father, to his mother, and to the relatives he had never known.

"Meena," the older girl started again, "remember the songs we sang with Papa? The ones we sang together?" Meena nodded her head gingerly. "Like the songs we sang in harmony, so, too, is a single life sung in harmony with all of life. You cannot hear Papa singing, but his song continues. Only his voice cannot be heard."

"Papa is not alive?" Meena asked as if she were unsure.

"Papa is not alive," her sister echoed. "But even though he has stopped singing with us, his song does not cease to be. Nature will give him another song to sing one day — one that can be heard again in this world."

Hakim interrupted softly. "What do you mean by that? Your father will not come back." Hakim did not intend to be mean, but he wanted to clarify the idea for himself.

"Not in his same form, no." Devi lay her hand gently on her sister's hair. "But life does not cease to be just because it changes form."

Devi looked at Hakim with tender eyes. The soothing tone of Devi's voice and the simple wisdom in what she was saying kept the other two nodding.

Meena looked at her sister hopefully. "Can Papa come back to us?"

"He will not come back. He will not walk beside us again," Devi said assuredly. "But we can give him prayers, we can give him attention in our own hearts, and he will return it to us. If we give him love the way we always have, then the love shall be returned."

"Is that so?" Hakim was surprised to find himself asking.

"Love is never wasted. Love always breeds love." Devi looked at him. "And hate breeds hate. Our experience of life will reflect what lies inside us. What we give to others is what we receive. My father once told me that giving is the instrument through which life sings. And receiving is also necessary or the song will not be heard."

Hakim nodded. Devi turned to her sister and held her hand. Next to the pile of ashes, the girls' mother was being helped to her feet.

"My father gave me this when I was my sister's age," said Devi. Hakim watched Devi reach behind her neck to unclasp a shiny brown necklace. "These are goldstones. In the old palaces the kings set them into the walls of their wives' chambers to create a reflection of their beauty. Take it." She turned to Hakim, the necklace in her hand.

"I cannot . . ." he said, stunned that the girl would offer him such a treasure.

"Yes, you can. You must." She dropped it in his hands.

"Do you have a papa?" Devi asked, without shifting her gaze from the pyre.

"I do not have a mother or a father," Hakim replied. "I have looked for a long time."

"Where did you look?" she asked.

"Everywhere," he answered without hesitation.

"Everywhere?" she repeated. "Both far and near?"

"Both far and near," he replied, mimicking her.

"How near?" she asked, undaunted. *"Not within,"* she whispered to herself.

"How? . . ." He did not understand her.

"I will give you one more thing." She turned to him and stared into his eyes. He was drawn in by her serious tone. "There's a small village a few hours to the east. There is someone there you must meet who may help you to find your parents . . . or whomever you are looking for."

Before Hakim could respond, Devi rose, pulling her younger sister with her. "Come on, Meena." The two girls started back toward their mother.

Hakim looked down at the string of stones he

held in his hands. He clutched it tightly and thought of what he must do.

In the distance Devi was brushing the dirt from her clothing, and Meena was following her example, wiping her own clothing with her tiny hands. Hakim didn't notice the smile of the woman who stood sweeping the ground. He only saw the flash of a green jewel on her right hand as it caught the sunlight.

Hakim looked again at the delicate necklace. The little beads shimmered in the sunlight as he reached behind his neck to put it on. The two girls had almost reached their mother and the holy man who was chanting prayers and sprinkling flowers on the ashen pyre.

Meena began to question her sister again, but Devi caught her before she started. "Stay silent, Meena . . . and cry."

9

WHEELS OF POWER

AFTER HIS ENCOUNTER WITH MEENA AND DEVI, Hakim spent the afternoon lost in thought. He wondered about their loss, how the lives of the two girls would change without their father. He thought about his own life and what it would be like to have a father to guide him. Usually when he thought of such things, Hakim felt sorrowful and lonely. But now he just wondered, allowing his mind to drift.

That day, as Hakim walked through the bazaars and markets, he imagined that his own father was there beside him. To his amazement, he actually created an image of his father. For fleeting moments he felt him there. In his mind and heart, he had created a father who loved him.

But now he had lost the feeling of being loved. It was swallowed up somewhere inside him. Hakim wasn't angry or anxious about it. He had only one thought: how and where he could reclaim that special feeling. This brought him back to what Devi had told him. *To the east,* he recalled her words. He reasoned that the wise one was probably in one of the countless villages toward the desert. So it was to the east he turned and started walking.

Hakim reached the outskirts of the city, where the rural plains stretched to the horizon and only ancient living villages spotted the landscape. The truck stop, amidst the dust and dirt and dry night air, reminded him of watering holes where camels filled up before journeying into the endless desert. The only ones drinking anything here, however, were the truck drivers who fortified themselves with alcohol for the long, all-night voyages ahead.

The thunder of passing trucks rolled by. They were colorful and loud, with pictures of dancing Gods ornamenting their sides and words inscribed on the hoods of their engines.

Hakim looked at the trucks pulled over on the side of the road. He could see their heavy cargo tightly packed to squeeze as much as possible into their boxes and flatbeds. They looked vulnerable, as if they might topple over at any moment. But when they raced by, they were sturdy as speeding tanks rushing toward enemy lines.

Hakim sat beneath a tree where he could watch the trucks parked on the far end of the road leading to the eastern plains. He listened to the chatter and laughter as the truckers entertained one another with tales of their recent exploits. Bright lights from passing trucks gave the appearance of a staged drama as the truckers vigorously waved their hands all about.

The area was lit with lanterns hanging from nearby trees, but the light barely revealed the pensive look on Hakim's face. His thoughts were focused on the path to freedom and happiness — his search for the secrets of the wise one.

Behind Hakim was a decrepit wooden shack, under which a man stood over a rudimentary stove. A fierce fire burned below a blackened tin bowl full of seething yellow oil that itself appeared to have been there for centuries. The man dipped rough balls of dough into the oil, watching it sizzle and crackle for a few seconds before flipping the biscuits onto a filthy counter. A number of drivers gathered around to wait for their last meal before departing.

A young boy, smaller than Hakim, shot back and forth between the counter and the truckers, bearing food to the men who greedily reached out for it. Every so often, a driver would belch loudly, signifying that he was ready to leave.

Hakim watched a wiry-framed trucker order the little boy to fetch another fried biscuit. The boy obediently obliged. Hakim, almost hidden in the shadows, peered at the man carefully. He was small and skinny. His skin was dark and shining with the same luster as the oily biscuits being served. His head, completely bald, reflected the moonlight. Black eyes, narrow lips, and a broad flat nose dominated his sharp face. He was frowning until he noticed Hakim staring at him.

The driver swallowed his biscuit quickly and slowly stood up. He spread his arms backwards, arched his body, and yawned loudly. Then he turned and nodded to the cook, handing him a few coins. Hakim watched as he headed toward his waiting truck. The wiry trucker peered into the shadows, finding Hakim's small, crouched figure. His dark eyes fixed on the boy.

"Come on then, friend, need a lift?"

Taken aback by the man's directness, Hakim didn't know how to respond. He stared at the man.

"Are you gonna just sit there watching the world pass you by?" The trucker appeared to chuckle to himself. "Not such a bad thing I suppose, but now is not the time." His expression became stern. He turned and started walking toward one of the large orange trucks parked half on the dirt, half on the road.

"Come on then," he yelled without looking over his back.

Hakim got up slowly and started toward the truck.

"I'm not exactly sure where I'm going," Hakim said after he had hoisted himself into the cabin and seated himself next to the small, dark man.

"Not exactly sure." The man mimicked Hakim's tone. "Those are strange words from someone your age. Might make me start wondering why I'm not *sure* where *exactly* I'm going either."

"I mean," Hakim began again, "I'm not sure where you can take me."

The man responded quickly, "I cannot take you anywhere, friend. Only you can do that. My advice to you — and I have been down this road many times before — is to concentrate on the journey and not the destination. This road we travel on tonight has many exits to many other roads. If you concentrate on all those other roads, you sacrifice your attention to the moment you are living right now. That is a burden — a burden you do not need. When the other roads present themselves, that is the time to make a choice. Not now."

He ended his speech by cranking the engine and thrusting the gear shift back. The engine roared and exhaled thick black smoke as if it were a dragon being released from captivity. The truck jolted forward and rolled off the dirt onto the road, picking up speed with every second.

The inside of this cabin is just as colorful as the outside, Hakim thought as he inspected his surroundings. Yellow, red, and green ribbons lined the paneling all over the inside. Little golden bells similar to the ones brides wear on their wrists at Indian weddings hung from the roof of the cabin.

Two small pictures were pinned on the dash, just over the gear shift. One was of a handsome blue-skinned God dancing and wielding a flute between his delicate hands. The other was of a green, unsightly demon, bearing a mace in one hand and choking a serpent in the other. Hakim recognized them immediately. His imagination began to bring them to life with the stories and myths he had heard all his life. Right below the pictures in fancy red writing, Hakim noticed some words. He squinted his eyes with effort to read: *"Our thoughts, our words, and our deeds are the threads of the net which we throw around ourselves."*

"My name's Mustafa, friend," the man said, breaking the silence again.

"Hakim," Hakim responded, but he couldn't think of anything else to say. He struggled for a moment, "Are you from around here?"

Mustafa replied with a laugh, "No, I am from a land quite far away."

"Why did you come here?" Hakim asked innocently.

"This is where my path has brought me. We each have a duty to follow the path that is before us. I am from the westlands, many kingdoms and seas away, and I have traveled to this place because it is my duty to teach. That is what my ancestors have done, and that is the identity I carry within me. That is why I am here." The cabin settled into an uneasy silence.

The truck barreled forward at high speed, keeping them bouncing up and down. Only a thin tunnel of light made by the truck's headlights pierced through the dark night that insulated the road on either side.

Occasionally they would come upon another truck or a little car zipping along the road, causing Mustafa to swell with excitement. He enjoyed switching lanes, flashing his high beams, and using his horn to scare oncoming vehicles and warn the ones he passed.

Before long, they came upon an overturned truck on the side of the road. Mustafa flashed his lights on it, exposing the contents that had fallen out. Hakim followed it with his eyes, turning and looking back at the wreck as their truck rolled by.

"Payment of karmic debt," Mustafa muttered to himself.

"What's that?" Hakim asked.

"Payment for past karma," Mustafa repeated.

Hakim thought to himself. He had heard the word *karma*, but he realized that he didn't understand it. "What do you mean?"

Mustafa raised his eyebrows and grinned. "Karma is action. Every action has a consequence. Therefore, karma is action and consequence. That fellow" — he pointed with his hand to the truck they had just passed — "made a choice and took action based on that choice. He just experienced the consequence of that action."

"Perhaps he lost control of his truck," Hakim responded. "Perhaps there was something in the road he wanted to avoid and he tipped over his truck through no fault of his own."

Mustafa answered slowly. "Perhaps that was not the action to which I referred."

Hakim felt deflated and remained silent.

"The consequence of action does not always follow the action immediately, my friend. The result sometimes blossoms far after the seed of the action has been planted." Mustafa was silent for a moment to let his words sink in. "Each consequence in itself is another action. That fellow did not deserve to crash, but somewhere along the line he made a choice that led to it. The crash itself is another action that leads into the future, and now he must make another choice about how this accident will affect him. Will it strengthen him, or will it weaken him?" Mustafa paused for a moment.

"I once heard a wise man say that the best way to prepare for the future is to be completely attentive to the present — to the choices we make in each moment. When we are conscious of the choices we make in each moment, the future takes care of itself and the journey becomes more enjoyable."

Mustafa's mention of "a wise man" made Hakim's stomach jump, but he was curious about what Mustafa had said earlier. "You said it is a burden to focus on the future, on roads far from the one we are on."

"Indeed it is, friend," Mustafa replied. "We are not living this moment if our attention is consumed by the future or the past. When we live in the future, we invite fear. When we live in the past, we invite sorrow. But when we live in the moment, we invite excitement, enthusiasm, and innocent wonder."

Choices. Hakim thought about all the roads they had passed. "How do we know if we are making the best choice, choosing the best road?"

"The only way to do that, my friend, is to trust your heart, the voice of your intuition," Mustafa responded. "Too often we make choices based on the intellect alone, and we keep ourselves locked into the same pattern and routine. We relive the same experiences over and over again, afraid to take risks or to act on our dreams."

Devil. Hakim recalled Lamia's reading at the carnival.

Mustafa looked closely at Hakim. In the dim light of the cabin, he could make out Hakim's soft, boyish features framed by thick black hair that fell in little ringlets from his forehead. *So young,* he thought to himself.

"How can we trust what our heart tells us when there are so many roads to choose from?" Hakim asked pointedly.

"How can we not, Hakim?" Mustafa shot back, using Hakim's name for the first time. "Only the heart considers every probability, every possible outcome in the universe. Nothing is excluded; everything is accounted for. That is what enables it to guide us toward the right decision."

Hakim looked at the wiry truck driver who barreled his behemoth down the highway with little resistance from anything in its path. "How do we *know* it is the right choice?"

Mustafa smiled. "You will feel it."

"Feel what?" Hakim retorted.

"You will feel peace and comfort and no resistance from the universe. When you make the right choice, your body will let you know with a feeling of comfort. You will feel good. But if you make the wrong choice, you will feel that, too, as discomfort in your body.

"There is a common thread that weaves through each one of us, despite our differences. No matter what color, what sex, what age we may be, we are all united by the sisterhood and brotherhood of our humanity. Nothing can alter our common identity.

"I am from a land far from here, and yet you and I are made of the same stuff, the same spirit. It is called God. The spirit of God is in the heart of every being — "

Hakim interrupted, "What does God — ?"

Mustafa broke in, "No, no, no. God *does* not. God *is*. The presence of God can be found everywhere, in everything. The same spirit that runs through a blade of grass speaks to each one of us through our heart. When we listen and make choices based on its wisdom, we ultimately bring happiness to everyone."

The cabin was silent except for the rattling of various trinkets jostled by the bumps in the road. The truck barreled down the path with abandon. Hakim watched the road, looking at each exit as it passed by. *Surely these roads lead to many others.* He thought about the countless villages, knowing the wise one might be impossible to find.

Glancing at the two small portraits of the deities on the dashboard, Hakim switched his gaze from the playful God to the dark demon, looking for some sort of sign. Then he peered into the darkness above where stars still clung to the sky. They were clear and bright, unlike any he had ever seen in the city. He thought about the Master for the first time in a while. *If I never find the wise one, maybe I can still learn his secrets from the Master. . . .*

"Shan't help you," Mustafa remarked, staring at the road ahead.

"Who?" Hakim shot back, feeling that Mustafa was intruding into his thoughts.

"The stars, of course," Mustafa quickly responded. "If you're looking out there for answers, you won't find them."

Hakim leaned back in his seat.

Mustafa continued. "There are, for certain, forces that will try to influence you and the choices you make, but you alone have the power to make the right choices."

The right choices. A voice resounded in his head as he looked at one of the roads that intersected the highway.

"This one looks good." Hakim spoke with con-fidence.

"Indeed," Mustafa replied.

The truck pulled over and came to a halt on the dirt embankment. The faint light of early dawn was beginning to appear on the horizon. Not too far from where they stopped, a cloud of smoke rose gently to the sky, signaling a nearby village.

"Must be off." Mustafa's voice rang out inside the cabin. "This isn't my path. It is yours." He winked at Hakim. "See you, my friend." Hakim jumped out of the cabin and disappeared around the rear of the truck.

The engine roared again as it began to slowly roll forward. Hakim gave the bright orange truck one last glance, then turned and began walking toward the village.

Mustafa headed down the main road again, but his gaze was stuck in the side-view mirror. He was not looking at the boy, but at a woman wearing a white sari who stood beside the road. Her right hand looked as if a green star had fallen from the sky and landed on her finger. Just before she turned away, her eyes met the truck driver's in the mirror and acknowledged them with a warm, bright smile.

10

TEMPTATION

HAKIM ENTERED THE DESERT VILLAGE JUST AS DAWN was beginning to break and the village was waking with the familiar clatter of life. There was no road at all and few vehicles. A worn path served as the main artery through which everything came in and out of the village.

Hakim looked around and didn't see much activity or excitement. Cows, roosters, and vagrant dogs passed here and there. He was beginning to question why he had chosen this place, when a man at the far end of the path stepped out from the shadows.

"How is it, son?" Hakim turned to face the gentleman and saw a tall, wiry fellow.

"Fine," Hakim answered the man with confidence.

"Like a drink?" The man reached back into the shadows and pulled out a soaked bottle of soda. "The heat tends to get to you." He brushed his forehead with the back of his arm as if to suggest it was already sweltering.

Hakim felt a curious sense of distrust in the pit of his stomach, but he was tempted by the refreshing sight of the soda.

"I would, actually." Hakim was now standing next to the man who was up one step from the ground. He reached out for the drink.

"Uh uh," the man stepped back for a moment, grabbed a bottle opener, and proceeded to flick the cap off the bottle. He handed the icy soda to Hakim and motioned with his other hand at a chair half concealed in the shade.

Hakim sat down and started to sip the drink, noticing the flimsy wooden table between them. Hakim looked at the man's face. It was as jagged as if it had been carved with a chisel. His nose was long and slender, and his eyes squinted out from two small slits in his face. His mouth was small, and when he smiled a little scar led to a small black mole that clung to the side of his face. Hakim found himself staring at the mark for a moment, unable to understand why it bothered him so.

"What brings you to our little village?" the man started. "I have not seen you here before." He snapped a match with his fingers, ignited the end of his cigarette, and hurled the match to the ground.

"Looking for something? Someone?" He blew a trail of smoke into the air. "I might be of service in that case, you know."

Devi, Hakim thought silently to himself. *Is this the one I'm supposed to meet?* He paused for a moment to listen to his heart, remembering what Mustafa had told him.

"Just passing through," Hakim shot back at the man with a proud grin.

The man shuffled his feet, taken aback by the boy's response.

"And you are?" Hakim followed quickly.

The man faltered for a moment, as though not expecting the boy to be so forward. "Luh . . . Lucius." He regained his composure. "Name is Lucius, and you are, son?"

"Hakim." Again his reply was confident and quick. The man was annoyed by Hakim's youthful arrogance, but he pressed on.

"I might be able to save you some time. With my assistance, you might even get what you want without working too hard at it." He raised his eyebrows to accentuate his offer.

Hakim looked at him suspiciously. He wanted to believe Lucius could help him in some way. Perhaps the answer to his search for the wise one lay just on the other side of Lucius' offer. Hakim was tempted, but resistance welled up within him. Something did not *feel* right.

"I'm all right."

Lucius nodded slowly, acknowledging Hakim's decision to reject his help. "Well, if you're just passing through, I might just show you the best way out." Lucius stared at the boy holding his cigarette to the side.

"I'm quite all right," Hakim replied feeling more and more confident. "I might stop and rest a while in the shade."

"In the shade?" the man asked curiously.

"Yes, beneath the trees, where it's cool." Hakim pointed with his head toward a cluster of trees not far from where they sat.

The man fully regained his cool temperament. "Not afraid of the dark are you, boy?" He leered at Hakim through the swirls of smoke that emanated from his cigarette.

"No, I'm not." Hakim detected something ominous in the man's voice and was beginning to feel uncomfortable.

"I like that. I have always believed the dark is far more inviting. You can get away with a whole lot more in the dark." He fabricated a smile as he leaned back in his chair. "Now tell me again, boy, what is it you want? I'm sure I can show you where to find it." Lucius was bearing down on Hakim's increasing trepidation. His eyes glowed with a furious fire, as he now felt Hakim's curiosity laced with fear and desire.

Hakim listened intently to Lucius' words, avoiding his eyes.

Lucius capitalized on the silence. "Now don't be afraid to say what you want. There's nothing wrong with a desire for . . . might we say *power* or *money?*"

Hakim was stunned by his words. A turbulence began to spin inside his stomach. Selfishly, curiously, Hakim wanted to hear what the man had to say. But he remembered what Mustafa had told him, *Listen to your heart*, and he shifted his attention there. Hakim's heart was beating rapidly, almost uncomfortably so. *Is this what Mustafa was talking about?*

"I need to be going." Hakim spoke as he started from his seat. "Thanks for the drink." He bolted from the table and headed toward the main alley from which he had come.

"Yes," Lucius responded in a disheartened tone, his voice trailing Hakim. "Well, I'm *sure* I'll see you again sometime."

Hakim stumbled over his own feet, for part of him was still curious and tempted to stay. Then at once he understood what was boiling in his belly and making his heart race.

Hate breeds hate. Hakim thought of Devi's words as he struggled to control his feelings toward this man.

Lucius was standing at the edge of the shadow, which had since grown larger with the advancing light. "Yes, it does," he smiled and whispered to himself taking one last puff at his cigarette before hurling it into the dirt.

11

DANCE OF THE SPIRIT

HAKIM LEFT THE MAIN SQUARE AND HEADED TOWARD a cluster of wooden huts in the heart of the village, glancing over his shoulder to ensure Lucius wasn't behind him. He had the distinct impression he was being watched.

At the far end of an alley, Hakim spotted a large hut from which he could hear laughter. He approached it slowly, not certain whether the villagers inside would welcome him. As he drew closer, Hakim noticed a collection of small bicycles tossed on the ground near the doorway.

Quietly he peeked through the thin slit of light between the doorway and a straw curtain that loosely covered it. Inside was a young woman surrounded by — he counted quickly — seven girls sitting in a circle.

Some of the girls were not much younger than himself. They were all dressed in bright, loose clothing, wrapped in reds, yellows, greens, and blues. Streams of sunlight poured in from the windows, washing the room with brightness, as particles of dust danced in the light, only to disappear in the shadows. The hushed buzz of an oscillating fan gently moved the warm air across the room.

The children's faces were rapt with wonder as the young woman whispered theatrically, "I was terrified the first time I saw the Goddess Kali. She was as dark as midnight, her fiery red eyes spinning in all directions. Her tongue was stained with blood, and her forehead was marked with a crescent moon. A necklace of serpents and a garland of skulls hung around her neck. She wore corpses as earrings, and her belly jiggled as she balanced on the stomach of her fallen husband. *How could I dance for her?* I thought to myself."

The little girls huddled around the young woman nodded as she repeated, "How could I give my dance to this demon?"

"Then my grandmother, who was my teacher, told me that I must give my dance and give it with love and honor."

The girls gasped with surprise and horror. The youngest one burst out, "How could you, Neena aunty? How could you give your dance to such a dark creature? I could never."

"Darkness, child, is only another expression of light. Without one, we could not have the other. Just as darkness and light exist together, so do evil and goodness. If we refuse to acknowledge the shadows, how can we honor the light?" The woman was silent for a moment.

"Why can we not just ignore what is evil?" another girl asked.

"Evil, child" — the woman turned to her — "is the name we give it. How can we ignore what is a natural part of life, a part of our own existence?"

Some of the girls shuddered as one of them asked, "There is evil inside us?"

"There are seeds of evil inside us, just as there are seeds of divinity. We have to accept both." She continued with a tender voice, "What we call good or bad, beautiful or ugly, is merely a judgment. The moment we judge, we separate ourselves from a part of life and lose sight of the unity of all things. When we refuse to judge, our minds and hearts remain open to an infinite realm of possibilities." She smiled a radiant smile.

"Children, we live in a world of opposites, a world of contrast between many forces. There will always be light and darkness, good and evil, pain and pleasure, chaos and order. Only when we accept the world as it is and embrace the rich diversity of experience will we know true happiness and freedom.

"And now, I would like to start our dance lesson." The teacher rose as the seven girls nodded their approval, sprung to their feet, and prepared to dance.

"You're not doing it right," one of the little ones said in a hushed voice. "Concentrate."

"I am," the other one responded, rhythmically thumping her feet on the floor.

"That's still not right," the little girl insisted. "Try harder, Priya."

"I *am* trying."

She was interrupted by the teacher, who smiled tenderly at the two little girls. "Priya, trying is not the way." The girl who had been giving instructions flushed red in the face.

"What one does with too much effort becomes strained and difficult; what one does naturally and spontaneously flows smoothly and with ease." Her voice was soft and caring. "A flower does not try to bloom; it is the flower's nature to bloom. A fish does not try to swim; it swims without effort. So, too, a dancer must allow her inner nature to express itself in the dance."

The teacher tapped her feet on the ground, gently at first and then more forcefully. Her knees were bent and her back held straight. Priya began to follow her teacher's lead.

"Your point of reference must be your own self," the teacher said. She paused and looked at the little girls, thinking to herself that they were budding women. "You must not dance to impress others, or to seek their approval. No action is effortless if it is done for a response. You must dance to love and honor what is inside you."

The teacher turned, then started to dance with abandon, throwing her head back, twisting her body, and pounding her feet on the floor. The rhythm she started spread rapidly around the small room. Soon all the girls, led by the one named Priya, were dancing freely as a feeling of exhilaration flooded the room.

Hakim crouched in the shade beside the doorway and watched the girls begin to spin and dance in a whirling rainbow of colors. *They are beautiful*, he thought to himself.

They danced until their teacher stopped and moved to the far corner of the room. The girls quickly followed suit. They knelt before an assortment of miniature bronze Gods and Goddesses, some of which Hakim recognized. The girls clasped their hands together and echoed their teacher's brief chant.

Then the teacher leaned forward, picked up an oversized garland of flowers, and placed it over one of the statues, the most hideous of the lot. Kali. Hakim recognized it instantly as the Goddess the young woman had spoken of earlier.

The teacher backed away from the altar, her hands still clasped as she turned to the children. "Tomorrow."

The children rushed for the doorway amidst laughter and chatter, as Hakim struggled to his feet and dashed to the side of the hut so he would not be seen. The girls picked up their bicycles and headed for their homes in the village, leaving a trail of dust behind them.

Hakim stood there for a moment, wondering what to do. Quietly, he returned to the front of the hut and poked his head through the doorway. Just then, the teacher turned and caught Hakim peeking in at her. Embarrassed, Hakim considered running away, but he didn't move. He stood breathless, enchanted by the young woman's presence.

"Would you like to come in?" she asked, pulling at the clips that held her hair.

Hakim stepped forward timidly. The teacher turned away, drinking from a flask of water and wiping her forehead with a white towel. "A bit surprised as to why you're here, are you?" she asked.

"I'm looking for someone," Hakim said quietly.

"Looking for someone. Yes," she said softly. "My name is Neena. Perhaps I could be of some help." She turned toward him.

Hakim looked at her closely for the first time. She was beautiful. Her eyes were deepset and dark brown; her face was a study in delicate elegance. Her long dark hair, released from the clips, flowed onto her shoulders and down her back. She was slender and tall, her posture straight and proud. Hakim was fearful of taking his eyes off her lest she go away.

"Before we find this person you are looking for, tell me first," — she paused and smiled — "who are you?"

Hakim stammered for a moment, remembering his encounter with Maloney. "I . . . I am Hakim."

"Yes," she smiled. "Yes, you are! And who is Hakim?"

He thought about her question. He wanted to please her with his response, but could think of nothing to say.

Neena walked toward him. "Come, let us go see." She took his arm and led him into another, smaller room. It was dark inside, and the smell of jasmine permeated the thick, moist air.

Hakim's eyes slowly adjusted. After a moment he could see Neena kneeling in front of another collection of statues. She straightened and turned to him.

"Come, sit here." Neena motioned to a straw mat similar to the one she was kneeling on. Then she reached out and lit a tall red candle.

In its light Hakim could see a large wooden statue that dwarfed the others behind it. Hakim recognized it immediately as Krishna. He had always been fascinated by the mischievous prankster God.

Neena looked at him and smiled. "Close your eyes, and be silent for a moment."

Hakim shut his eyes.

"If thoughts come, let them come. If thoughts go, let them go." Neena spoke softly. "We give different names to the forces we feel."

Hakim listened carefully.

"We call love by different names: mother, father, God. . . . " Neena looked at the statue in front of them. "But we cannot forget where our true devotion must be." She paused. "The *self*. The height of devotion is to have a passionate love for who you really are. Who you really are is inseparable from the force that exists within everything around you. Express love, then, at every moment to whatever is around you, and you shall become the *beloved* . . . you shall always *feel loved*."

Neena continued after a brief pause. "I give my devotion at every moment to the seeds of divinity within me, to the presence of the deity within everyone. I give it in my dance, and in my love of teaching."

Hakim remembered what Devi had said. *Love always breeds love.*

Neena spoke again. "Freedom and happiness come effortlessly to those who can reconcile the many contradictions of life: the divine and the diabolical, the sacred and the profane. When one can comfortably flow between the banks of pleasure and pain, experiencing them both without getting stuck in either, then there is freedom."

She waved her hands. "I am Kali, and I am Krishna. I am noble, and I am wretched. I am beautiful, and I am ugly. I am dark, and I am light. I am the divine spirit that creates all of these. You are, too, Hakim." Neena looked at him and smiled warmly.

He felt his head floating as if it was no longer connected to his body. "This is who you are — all of these things and more, Hakim." Her voice stirred something within him. "Once you understand who you are, the universe will unfold its secrets to you. The wisdom you seek will be yours." Hakim nodded as he felt a peaceful calm wash over him.

"The path of least resistance is the path of love, harmony, and joy. Accept each moment as it is. The present moment is the doorway to both the past and the future. Do not resist it. If you struggle against this moment, you struggle against the past and the future."

Neena's voice echoed in his awareness until he lost his sense of time and space completely. Hakim felt only peace as he drifted into a weightless, sleeplike trance.

Suddenly he was aware of everything all at once: the dampness of the room, the mingled smell of incense and dust, the hum of the fan twisting in the next room, the sound of a vagrant dog fishing through the rubbish outside, the distant call of a crow perched high in a tree, the whispers of young lovers passing through the desert village.

Hakim's eyes were closed, but a brilliant flash of colors filled his inner being as if every cell in his body was rejoicing with renewed life. He became aware of being aware, as exhilaration raced through his body.

Hakim opened his eyes and found that he was alone. Neena was gone. Next to the door on a small table was a note addressed to him in elegant writing. He picked it up and read it out loud:

To Hakim, my Child of the Dawn:

You have awakened to the one you seek. Each of us is guided by the light of a Guardian Spirit. It is our own Self which watches over us, protects us from harm, and guides us toward the fulfillment of our dreams. Your light, your spirit, is strong, Hakim. Trust its guidance and follow your heart. You will always be welcome in my home. Until we meet again, I will hold you in my heart.

Always with love, Neena

Hakim peeked between the straw covering and the doorway and saw Neena dancing. There was no music playing, but she was spinning round and round, energized by a feeling of ecstasy that filled the room. After one last glance at her enchanted dance, Hakim left the small village without looking back.

On his way he noticed two birds sitting near a tree. One was stark white except for its eyes, which sparkled like bright green jewels. The other was a peacock that suddenly rose and spread its tail to reveal a dazzling display of luminous blue and green feathers. Hakim looked closely at the creature, admiring its beauty and poise. A voice emerged from the center of Hakim's being: *I am with you, Hakim. I will guide you.* The voice felt comforting and familiar. Hakim smiled warmly at the peacock, then turned and continued on his way.

12

RESTLESS WINDS

"YOU LEAD A CHARMED LIFE, YOU REALLY DO." THE round man placed his teacup on the coaster that lay on the table between them. His eyes were fixed on the elegant tapestries that hung on the walls, on the hand-made rugs that lay on the floor. "How do you do it?"

The Master's attention was elsewhere, but he thought about the question the man had posed. He looked over at the governor. Titles didn't mean much to the Master. What he saw was a fat, greedy man who couldn't see beyond the luxuries of rugs and wall hangings. To the Master, this man was not unlike a hungry animal begging for a morsel that might be tossed its way.

"Yes, I do." The Master spoke with little emotion. "I do lead a charmed life."

"But how do you do it? Tell me," the governor asked.

"I work" — the Master paused for a moment to accentuate his point — "hard." The room was growing dark, the lights were off, and there was an uneasy silence when the impetuous guest wasn't chattering away.

The governor was not satisfied. "Tell me if I am right. Those I know who have power and money, they are either the very good, the benevolent types, or the very bad — the merciless, the cunning, the cutthroat and corrupt. Am I right?"

"I suppose." The Master responded indifferently to what the man surmised was a profound insight.

"And which are you?" the governor quickly followed.

The Master looked at him sharply. "I ascribe to a philosophy that does not confine me to either of these types. My power is beyond your definition of good and bad. I am successful in my affairs because I understand how to take action with my desires and intentions fully in mind. That is my secret to power and wealth.

"These belongings of mine" — the Master pointed at all the luxurious items that filled the room, Persian rugs, oriental vases, and hand-carved furniture — "could come or go. They are nothing but symbols of my power. The wealth I enjoy is the result of the right use of power, not the source of it. All of us have power, but few of us understand how to use it."

The Master's thoughts turned to Hakim and his search for the secrets of the wise one. He thought of why he wanted him, needed him, in fact, as his student. But where had the little rascal gone? The Master would put the word out to his people on the streets. Soon he would know where to find the boy.

"I must go." The Master started from his chair.

The governor was bewildered by the Master's spontaneous oration. He hadn't understood a word, but nevertheless he was profoundly impressed and envious.

The Master looked at him, feeling sorry for the ignorant wretch.

"Shanti," he called out. The small servant scurried out from one of the doorways to the dark spacious room like a disciplined mouse. "Get my friend another cup of tea and whatever else he would like."

He turned back to the feebleminded man who remained still and in awe of the Master. "Stay and enjoy my hospitality. I must go. There is a young boy who needs my help."

"Needs your help?" The heavy-set man was instantly curious.

"Yes, he's one of the orphans who ran away two years ago." The Master began to pace back and forth with his hand on his chin.

"He is one of the few ambitious boys I know. He could actually help me manage my affairs, unlike my spoiled son, who is apparently more interested in drinking and gambling."

"Ah, I have heard about your troubles with Karun. How disappointing it must be for a man of your stature." The governor seemed to revel in this one flaw in the Master's life that was not so easy to correct.

"Well, this boy won't disappoint me. Once he hears my offer, he will be happy to work for me. But it's time he receives the proper cultivation." The cunning look on the Master's face was barely visible in the dim light.

The governor was silent except for the sound of his heavy breathing, which echoed around the empty space between them.

The Master spoke as if he had forgotten his visitor altogether. "Yes, he needs the proper cultivation," The Master smiled, "but not from these 'benevolent types' as you so aptly called them. They would merely confuse him with the idea of *goodness*." He ridiculed the word *goodness* with the tone of disgust in his voice.

"This child needs a mentor." He paused for a moment, unable to suppress the smile that slowly spread across his face. "He needs a wise one like me."

Hakim left the small village knowing something crucial had just occurred. He was beginning to realize the futility of his efforts to find someone he knew only as the "wise one." There were hundreds of villages and little possibility that the man who shared his secrets with the Master would appear years later to share them again. For that matter, Hakim wondered if there ever really was a wise one.

There should have been sadness or disappointment in this realization, but strangely there was not. Hakim knew his search for the wise one had not been in vain. Although he had not discovered any secrets to power, Maloney, the storyteller, Lamia, Devi, Mustafa, and Neena — all had shared their wisdom with him. The material wealth he longed for was still a distant dream, but he had learned some important keys to happiness.

For the first time in his life, Hakim felt the lost, empty feeling leaving his body; an inner calm was taking its place. A new life was growing in the depths of his soul. The note from Neena only reinforced what he was beginning to understand. Somewhere, hidden within his own heart, was the purpose for his life. There was a special place for him, if only he knew what it was.

13

FLAMES OF DARKNESS

DAYS HAD PASSED SINCE HAKIM HAD SLEPT FOR ANY length of time. Now he felt a weariness throbbing inside, propelling him into a heavy slumber. He could barely stay awake as he searched for a place to lie down and sleep.

Wearily, he made his way to the outskirts of the village, where a truck sat parked on the side of the road facing west. It was dusk and the sun had set, leaving an orange glow on the land. Hakim could see the driver standing under a tree, with his back toward him. The man was chatting to himself as a thin funnel of smoke from his cigarette swirled in the air and formed a cloud above his head.

Hakim was hesitant to approach the man. Instead, he slipped unnoticed past the driver to the back of the truck, where he hoisted himself into the trailer. He landed with a hollow thud on the wooden planking that made up the base of the trailer's floor.

The space was sparsely packed compared to other trucks he had seen. Hakim slid behind a large container and tried to push it aside with his hands. It wouldn't budge. Confident that the weight wouldn't shift, Hakim lay down and was spiraling into a deep sleep before the truck shifted into gear and rumbled off toward the city. His chest barely moved with each breath, as if a heavy weight sat upon him, confining him to the images that danced across his mind.

Hakim dreamed he was wandering around a small

shop filled with wax candles of every color and size. Bright, exotic candles took the shape of different animals: purple cows, orange cats, red cobras. Many of the candles were lit, giving the small store a warm yellow glow.

Hakim looked around, enjoying the beauty of the flickering candlelight. Everything was soft, hushed, and slow, reminiscent of the mood in a cathedral or mosque. The strong, almost sensuous silence was broken by the delicate ringing of wind chimes.

Hakim looked out a window and noticed that night had fallen; he felt the sharp contrast between the warm yellow light in the room and the cold blackness outside.

"May I help you find something?"

Hakim turned to see an exotic-looking man sitting behind a wooden desk, its elegant paneling shined to a golden luster. The man was casually flipping through the pages of a magazine.

"Is there something special you are looking for? *Someone* perhaps?" Hakim was about to answer when the man's face suddenly changed. Now he was the

Master, staring at Hakim with an eerie smile on his face. Hakim was not as terrified as he thought he would be. He was surprised at the Master's sudden appearance, but he quickly regained his composure.

"Oh, I know there is *something*," the Master continued. "How fortunate that I am here and able to help you find it."

Hakim studied the Master's face. Somehow, he looked different. He had the same handsome face, but something about him had changed. *It is something in his eyes*, Hakim thought.

The Master grinned. It was a contrived, sweet smile, the one the Master used when he wanted a favor. Hakim suddenly felt restless and uncomfortable, but found himself unable to move, as if a heavy weight sat upon him.

"You have come far, Hakim. I would say you've come to the right place to find who you are looking for. Let me help you find the wise one. Remember, it was I who started you on this journey toward wisdom and power."

Before the boy could respond, the Master grabbed his arm and led him through endless winding aisles that became a labyrinth of passages. The Master moved easily, as if he knew the way. They were descending. Hakim looked for steps, but found only a smooth path.

"Where are we going?" Hakim asked after a while, disturbing his own silent wonder.

The Master chuckled. "You bring me here and then ask me where we are going? You invite me into your own imagination, the confines of your own soul, and ask such foolish questions?" He laughed again. "That's very funny, Hakim. That's really very funny."

Hakim continued to follow the Master through the darkness until, finally, he stopped short.

"Well, Hakim, you are ready to learn something." The Master turned and faced him. "It is not until we are ready to learn that the perfect teacher appears."

Hakim stared at him, not understanding the Master's comment.

"Looks good, doesn't it, boy?" The Master looked around at the surrounding darkness as he leaned in closer to Hakim. "A bit dark, but it suits me fine." He smiled and reached over to grasp a thin string that appeared from nowhere. He pulled on it, and suddenly a new set of scenery replaced the darkness. They were standing outside amidst seven large gray stones that formed a circle around them. Sitting atop the stones were the same candles he had seen before, flickering in a light breeze.

"Well, then," the Master said. "You have longed to know the secrets to wealth and power, Hakim, and I have decided to share them with you. In return, I ask only that you come to work for me, so you might put your newly found knowledge into practice."

Hakim was quiet.

The Master spoke in a seductive whisper, but his words were crystal clear. "When you begin to understand the world as an extension of your own self, of your own thoughts and feelings, then you will understand that you have the power to change it. Therein lies the key to true power, Hakim."

Hakim nodded, entranced by the Master's voice.

"Essentially, you and I, these rocks, the candles you see, we are all made from the same stuff." He pointed to the candles, which had burned into dark- and light-colored soups of all shades. "We all consist of the same basic components: oxygen, hydrogen, nitrogen, carbon, and other elements in small amounts."

Hakim stared at the Master, unable to focus on anything but the mole next to his right eye.

"My point is, Hakim," the Master started again, "the ingredients are all the same. The difference is in how we use them. Each one of us is responsible for creating our own world. The world we experience is a product of our own perception, our own creation."

Having delivered this wisdom, the Master smiled. He opened the palm of his hand to reveal a blue and green candle in the shape of a globe. The Master knew that magic would stir the boy. He closed his hand again and jerked his arm to his side. On the rock to their side the candle appeared with its wick ablaze.

"Follow me?"

Hakim shook his head. "How can I create one world, and you create another, when we are all living in the same world? I do not follow."

The Master's smile widened. "Where does my body end and yours begin, Hakim? Since we are made of the same stuff, then what gives us a different experience of the world is the way we perceive the ingredients — what we do with them in our own awareness. By changing our beliefs, our perceptions, we cause our experience to change, and in this way we change the world around us. There is no true boundary or limit to the self; there is no separation from the world that encircles us. When we master the forces within, we influence the forces without." He grinned from ear to ear. "Do you see the possibilities, Hakim? The power we can command?"

Hakim nodded, still enchanted by the Master's voice.

"Listen to me carefully now," he said, looking at Hakim with a stern face. "Thought mixed with feeling is a powerful force; it has tremendous energy. This is a little known secret of power. Whatever we think about gains energy from our attention — it grows larger in our life. If we take our attention away from something, it loses power and importance. Do you see how we create our own world by changing our perception, our own awareness? Whatever we choose to focus on — scarcity or abundance, empowerment or impoverishment — is drawn to us."

Hakim looked puzzled. "I can have whatever I want just by thinking about it?"

"Not by thought alone, Hakim. Attention is important, but intention and action are also necessary. You must be clear about what you want and willing to take action to get it. Intention orchestrates an infinity of details to bring about your desires. Intention is the magic, but action is necessary to activate it. That is why I have chosen you as my protégé. My own son could not understand this principle. He is lazy and unwilling to do much of anything.

"Intention, attention, and action are the mechanics of the fulfillment of desire. Apply this knowledge, and whatever you want can be yours." The Master fabricated his sweet smile again. "I have known you all your life, Hakim. Like other boys your age, you want freedom, you want power, you want luxuries only money can buy. You can have all of these, Hakim. Everything you've ever wanted and more."

Hakim nodded, and thought about the Master's offer. He was tempted to learn from the Master and eager to hear the wise one's secrets, but he was distrustful of the Master's charming manner. Fear lingered within him like the smoke from burning ash, an apprehension he could not extinguish and was strangely leery of. Hakim was about to respond when he felt the air around them brighten. The Master looked up, too. The circle of rocks was gone, and they were suddenly inside the candle shop.

The Master was back behind his desk. There was a loud rattling at the door. They both looked to see who it was — the Master with irritation, and Hakim with innocent wonder.

A young woman, her features obscured by a dark

hood, was peering through the window on the door. Again she rapped on the glass panes with a ring that adorned her finger. Hakim stared at the brilliant green emerald gleaming with beauty against her light olive skin. Something about the ring reminded Hakim of a distant dream. Somehow that ring always appeared on the finger of a mystical loving presence that comforted and consoled him. Hakim almost felt as if he were being watched, protected, even guided to make the right choices.

The Master looked at the door with irritation, but managed to manufacture a cordial smile. He yelled out, "I'm sorry, madam, we're closed."

"Tell her we're closed, boy," he ordered Hakim. Then he noticed the ring. Now he could not conceal the fact that he was upset.

Hakim started toward the door.

The Master shouted, "I'm not finished with you yet." He shot a glance toward the door where the woman kept knocking with her ring.

Hakim was almost at the door.

"Boy, I'm not through. I haven't yet taught you all that you need to know."

The woman in the doorway smiled triumphantly at the Master, then tenderly at Hakim. She did not wait for Hakim; she slipped away just before he reached the door to unlatch it. When he opened the door, she was gone. The streets were empty and quiet. Where she had stood was a single candle. It was solid white and softly illuminated by the glow of a flickering flame.

Hakim stared at the candle for a moment, then reached out to touch it. A sudden jolt startled him and threw him backward. Then a rumbling noise like distant thunder filled his ears. He opened his eyes to find his arm outstretched, reaching for the full moon that had risen high above in the midnight sky.

Hakim lay tucked away in the back of a moving truck. Just before closing his eyes again, he looked once more at the moon. *It really doesn't seem that far away*, he thought as he returned to the world of his dreams.

14

SILENT SEA

HAKIM WOKE UP AS THE TRUCK ROLLED TO A STOP.
The position of the sun told him he had slept too long.
Where am I? Glancing around outside the trailer, he
saw a roadside village not unlike others he had seen,
except for its conspicuous lack of noise and activity.

The door to the truck's cabin was open, but the
radio was no longer playing. There was only silence.
Suddenly Hakim felt completely alone. He looked
around, hoping to find the driver, but saw no one at all.

Hakim jumped down from the trailer and stared at the empty streets. The little village felt like a graveyard. He noticed a gentle breeze rustling the branches of a tree. Then he noticed a salty tang in the air. Listening closely, he could hear the rhythmic pounding of waves against the shore.

Just as Hakim was about to make his way toward the beach, he heard something stirring in one of the abandoned buildings. *That must be the truck driver,* he thought, grateful for the company. A few steps led him to an open building with empty containers strewn about the floor. Inside, he only heard the wind knocking loose wooden planks.

Suddenly a woman emerged from a back door. She stumbled into the room, kicking one of the empty containers as she caught her balance. The two stared at each other for a moment in awkward silence. She wore white baggy pants and a loose white top. Her eyes were bright and her smile was engaging.

"Huh . . . hello," she stuttered.

"Hello," Hakim echoed.

"I'm afraid if you've come for someone, they've all gone away," she said.

"Gone where?" Hakim found himself asking.

"Gone to a nearby village . . . for now." She responded. "Suppose we'll move on from there in a couple of days, find some place more permanent to settle."

"And leave this place?" Hakim asked curiously, not exactly knowing where this place was.

"We already have," she said with a slight chuckle. "I'm just back to collect a couple of things."

"Where are we? Why is this place abandoned?"

"We're up the coast about seventy miles from . . . you know where you are! You just arrived by truck." She pointed in the direction of the truck parked outside. "The fishermen have left town for more productive waters." She paused. "Since fishing has been the only industry here for as long as I can remember, there's really nothing left." She looked at Hakim. "Couldn't feed ourselves. People were starving."

Hakim looked at her blankly, not knowing what to say.

"Nothing you can do, really. One day the fish are gone. That's the way nature works. Can't change it." She kept looking at him.

Hakim found himself wanting to say that perhaps there was a way to change it, but the words would not come easily, so he remained silent.

The woman smiled. "There's an old man." She pointed out the door toward the ocean. "He's decided to stay. He's a bit wacky, but he might be able to help you find whoever you are looking for."

Hakim turned to leave.

"This evening we will have one last ceremony here with the elders to say goodbye to the village," she said. Hakim wondered if she was inviting him, but she didn't say another word. Instead she continued to pick up her things from the ground, then turned toward the door she had entered.

Hakim called out to her, "My name is Hakim."

She turned to him and smiled. "Mine is Maya."

The old man was sitting beneath a weather-bleached tarpaulin that shielded his slender body from the scorching sun. His back was bent slightly and his thin legs, swinging back and forth like a child's, hung over the edge of an old wooden dock. His bald head glistened with little beads of sweat.

Hakim approached the old man cautiously, but as soon as he was near him, Hakim felt a sense of warmth drawing him closer. His trepidation faded away.

The old man turned to Hakim and greeted him with a gentle, unassuming smile. "Hello, boy. Sit if you'd like." He pointed to the space beside him. "Would you like to try your hand at fishing?"

The old man gently threw his line out into the sea. The handmade fishing rod looked frail, as did the string that stretched into the water. Hakim shifted his feet and glanced around.

Very odd, Hakim thought. *There are no bait, no buckets or nets . . . not one captured sea creature.*

The old man handed him the rod, and Hakim took it, but only out of a desire to be polite. Just as he was beginning to wonder what he was doing in an abandoned village, seated next to an old man, fishing with a stick and string, Maya's word's echoed in his mind. *He might be able to help you find whoever you are looking for.*

The old fisherman chuckled quietly. "Ah, so I am to help you find someone you already know, is that it?"

Hakim was taken aback by the old man's sudden response to his thoughts.

The old man giggled as an innocent smile spread across his face. "What could I help you do? Who could I help you find? I am very old." He nodded his head as if to agree with himself. "I am only a fisherman."

Hakim interjected, "Then where do you keep the fish you catch?" He glanced around as if to prove the absence of a container.

"Oh no, I have never *caught* a fish." The old man responded with utmost sincerity.

Hakim looked at the man feeling more than slightly confused. "How is it that you call yourself a fisherman then?"

The old man took the rod from Hakim and threw the string out across the water. The mischievous grin returned. "I love the ocean. I love to sit here with my rod." He raised it slightly. "I love to fish, and so I am a fisherman."

"But why are you a fisherman if you do not catch fish?" Hakim was not convinced.

"Why must I *catch* fish to be a fisherman?"

"Have you ever eaten a fish that you caught yourself?" Hakim was now intrigued.

A smile spread across the old man's face, as if an epiphany had just been reached. "That must be it. I am a vegetarian. I do not eat fish, but I can still be a fisherman." The old man seemed relieved of some momentary anxiety.

Hakim was fascinated by the old man. Although he did not fully understand him, somehow he felt satisfied with the old man's explanation. *Could it just be the love of fishing . . .*

The old man looked kindly at Hakim, "Yes, it is the love of fishing that gives me reason to call myself a fisherman. Surely there is something that you love to do?"

Hakim could think of nothing in particular. He was silent and pensive as the old man continued.

"Now think carefully, and you will know what you love to do. Everyone has a special purpose, a special talent or gift to give to others, and it is your duty to discover what it is. Your special talent is God's gift to you. What you do with your talent is your gift to God."

"I don't know what my special talent is," Hakim said quietly. "Do you know what it is?"

The old man's voice became slow and steady. "What do you dream of doing, child? Your heart knows what this is, but you have not listened to the voice inside that tells you what is true." The old man smiled warmly at Hakim.

"I have dreamed that I was rich and powerful. I have dreamed that I have a father and mother of my own. How do I make these dreams come true?"

The old man paused for a moment, and then began again, "By believing in yourself, child. You must believe in your dreams and pursue them with love in your heart. Love is the key to the magical and the mysterious. It is a powerful force. When you love, your dreams find you. But first, you must believe in love, and you must believe in magic; otherwise, you bind yourself to the realm of the commonplace and mundane. That is the devil of your existence, child." He looked at Hakim with affection.

The old man had touched something deep within Hakim's mind. He began to recall his dream from the previous night. He remembered the Master teaching him about the secrets to power. Vague memories slipped in and out of his awareness: the warm glow of candles, the sound of wind chimes, the descending path, the Master's offer, the sparkle of a green emerald ring. . . .

The old man interrupted Hakim's contemplation. "Your last teacher, that unpleasant fellow," — the old man winced at the mention of him — "some of what he said is true, but he didn't tell you everything."

Hakim was wondering if the old man could read his thoughts. *He must be referring to the Master.*

"Yes, that is the one." The old man nodded. "He didn't tell you that those who are truly happy do what they love while also serving others. Wealth then comes in many forms. . . . Darkness lurks behind every corner; it will always try to tempt you. But do not confuse power and wealth with position and money alone."

The old man giggled and looked deep into Hakim's eyes. "What will make you truly wealthy is the joy you receive from giving your special gift to others. What will make you truly powerful is a heart filled with love — love for your self, for God, for every living and non-living thing, for life itself.

"I want to tell you a story." The fisherman changed his tone. His playful expression turned serious for a moment. "I am a storyteller as well as a fisherman. This is a story I'm fond of telling.

"There once was an old wise man who every day walked the same dirt path to his sister's home for afternoon tea. He carefully avoided the jagged rocks that could cut his bare feet and prevent him from continuing on his journey.

"At the same time each day, a younger man would also make the same journey on the path going the other way. This second man walked swiftly down the broken road in his luxurious leather shoes. In this way the two men passed each other every day.

"One day, where the two men usually crossed paths, a scorpion lay on its back, unable to turn on its feet. The younger man saw the older one bend down and turn the creature onto its legs to enable it to continue. Just as he turned it, the scorpion stung the man on the back of his hand. The young man, alarmed at the sight, rushed forward and stomped on the little creature. He then confronted the old man. 'I do not understand you! Are you a fool? Why do you touch a scorpion when you know that it will sting you?' The old man looked at the dying creature sadly and then at the man. 'And I do not understand you, for just as it is the scorpion's nature to sting, it is ours to love.'"

The old man stopped talking and stared into the sea. Having listened intently to the fisherman, Hakim quietly asked, "And what is my nature?"

"That is the choice you must make, child. The path of love is a choice you make in every moment." His voice was soft and tender.

Hakim turned to the fisherman, looking at him closely for the first time. Despite his old age, the fisherman's giggles and grins made him seem like a child. There was an irrefutable source of youth bubbling within him that permeated everything around him. Hakim felt this energy seep into him, filling his own awareness with bliss.

There was something soothing in the old man's voice, in this fisherman who didn't catch fish and liked to tell stories. Hakim felt his own heart blossoming as he realized what it was. *It was love. . . .*

"Are you known as the wise one?" Hakim asked quietly.

"I am very wise," the old man laughed and shook his head. "I have seen many things in my many days. But I am not the wise one you seek. The wise one you seek has been with you all along, right there beside you." The old man tapped Hakim's shoulder. "You have refused to see it, but that is not your fault. Wisdom does not spring from one fountain. Everything will reveal its secrets if you only love it enough. Look within your own heart for wisdom, my child. You are the maker of miracles when you believe in the magic."

The old man was quiet. He raised his head and faced the setting sun as if to feel the wisdom radiating from its light. He looked at the water as if to read an ancient script buried in the depths below its surface. He perked his ears as if to hear the whispers of the wind and the secrets it carried from faraway places.

The old man is in love with life, Hakim thought as he looked out across the ocean, searching that elusive place where the sky embraces the sea. The water had turned a colorful hue of bright orange to match the setting sun.

The old man slowly began to rise from his seat. "It is time for you to catch a fish." Chuckling, he stood and stretched the soreness from his legs.

"I once heard a story of a man who caught five thousand fishes," the old man said to Hakim with a glisten in his eyes. "He caught five thousand fishes and fed an entire village." He raised his eyebrows, as though impressed with the idea of such a feat. "Do you think I might catch that many fish? I think *you* could because you're so young and strong."

Hakim started to say something, but the old man interjected. "Our dreams are meant to come true, you know. What would be the purpose of dreaming if we could not fulfill our dreams?"

There was a sudden tug on his fishing rod, then it bowed with tension. A bright smile spread across the old man's face. He handed the rod to Hakim, who surprised himself by taking hold of it.

"Pull it in, boy," the old man said happily.

Hakim pulled on the rod until finally a wriggling fish emerged from the sea and flopped beside him. Hakim was caught up in the excitement, as he had never before gone fishing.

The old man looked at Hakim. "Now toss it back in," the old man ordered.

Hakim's face contorted with curious surprise. He

reasoned that he must not have heard the old man properly.

"Go on, throw it back in," the old man insisted.

"But why?" Hakim asked.

The old man gave Hakim an authoritative glance, the kind a father would give his boy.

Hakim tossed the silver fish back into the water and watched as it streaked away with renewed life.

"We do not need trophies to validate our worth," the old man began. "Neither you nor I have any need for that fish." He smiled. "I am a vegetarian, and you are not going to carry a smelly fish around with you." The old man laughed softly to himself.

Hakim thought of Maya and the people in the village. "What of those who do need it?"

"There are plenty of fish to feed them," the old man replied. "We only have to know how to ask in the proper way. First we plant the seed of our desire in the fertile ocean, then we must believe in our desire and expect the ocean to deliver." He pointed to the expanse of dark blue water in front of them.

The old man started to walk away, but Hakim followed.

"They are waiting for you, child."

Hakim wondered who the old man was referring to.

"Do you know what *Maya* means in Sanskrit?" The old man asked in a whisper, as if to share an important secret with him.

Hakim shook his head.

"Worldly illusion. Maya is the illusion that we live in a material reality. Maya is the mask of matter that hides the spirit." The old man giggled, and walked away.

Hakim stood thinking about the fisherman's words. *Plant the seed of our desire in the fertile ocean, then we must believe. . . .* The words sounded vaguely familiar to him. He thought of the village and the people who would have to abandon it. Hakim wished with all his heart that he could help them.

Just as he had this thought, his attention was roused by the sound of ringing bells. In the distance

Hakim could hear singing and chanting. The ceremony Maya had mentioned was well underway as the village people saluted goodbye to their home.

Hakim walked into the village and joined the crowd of people. He was searching for the woman named Maya, when suddenly he heard a shout. He turned to see a young boy no bigger than himself running up the path from the dock. In one hand the boy held a fishing rod and in his other hand a shiny tin bucket. The boy's words were unintelligible, but as he ran toward the villagers, one of the elders stopped him.

"What is it?" The old man asked.

The boy dropped his fishing rod and pointed into his bucket. Hakim looked and saw that the whole bucket was full of wet, silvery fish just like the one he had caught earlier.

The old man gasped, as did the other villagers, who quickly gathered around the young boy.

"There are hundreds, thousands," the boy shrieked, hardly able to contain his excitement.

"Where?" the elder man asked.

"Down by the dock," the boy answered quickly. "Come on!" He turned and dropped his bucket and waved his hand for the people to follow him. "The sea is full of them!"

The villagers quickly followed the boy, and Hakim stayed close behind them. When they reached the dock, Hakim saw the young boy standing exactly where Hakim had been with the old fisherman. He was pointing down into the water where Hakim had earlier thrown the fish back in.

The elder man was looking incredulously.

Hakim walked to the edge of the wooden planking and looked down into the water. People around him began to shout with excitement.

"They're real," one of them yelled, rubbing his eyes as if to make sure the sight would not disappear.

"It's a miracle," an older woman cried. Then she reached her hands toward the sky and began to chant, praising the grace of God.

Hakim looked out into the water again. The

ocean's surface was lined with silver. *There are millions of fish*, he thought to himself.

Hakim watched in silent amazement. Nobody seemed to notice him, immersed as they were in celebrating the renewed life of their village. Seeing the jubilant people made his heart leap with joy. For the first time ever, Hakim felt he was a part of something special. He knew he had played an important role in the revival of the village, although he could not explain how.

Off in the distance, another figure was watching Hakim. The boy turned and felt the old man's eyes on him. The fisherman was holding the frail rod in his hand, and for the first time Hakim noticed the green glint coming from a ring on his finger.

A voice echoed in Hakim's head: *Believe in your dreams. I will always be with you.* Hakim squinted his eyes and stared into the distance where the fisherman had been only moments before. The old man was no longer there.

15

PRELUDE OF THE NIGHT

THE CELEBRATION WAS AT ITS PEAK WHEN HAKIM walked away from the tiny village. With his search for the wise one at an end, Hakim was ready to return to the city where his journey had begun. Now he knew that his destiny awaited him, probably in some corner of a street he had passed a thousand times before. That much he had learned: that wisdom exists within everyone and everything, within every nook and cranny of the world.

It was well past midnight, and the full moon had risen high into the sky. The roads were empty. Hakim decided to find his way to the railroad station, where he could sneak onto a train heading toward the city.

Countless times, Hakim had hidden in the crowded trains until he could slip on the roofs of the cars where the luggage was stowed. He would bury himself between bags that were often bigger than he was, and ride the train for free. The conductors knew he was there, along with a dozen like him, but they reasoned it was better to let them sit on the roof than ride in the cabins where they might make trouble.

The train station, even at this time of night, was lively. A train pulled in, and Hakim slipped aboard. In the moonlight Hakim watched as others joined him on the roof, tucking themselves into warm, snug positions.

Hakim leaned his head back, letting it rest on one of the soft bags behind him. He looked into the vast night sky, where silver specks of stars hung in the moonlight. He wished he could make sense of all that he had learned, but he was tired and wanted to sleep.

"So we meet again," the voice rang out with familiar cheeriness. "It's good to see you, Hakim."

Hakim looked up and saw the pleasant face and smile of Maloney, the magician, who was walking across the roof of the train.

"Mind if I join you?" Maloney looked down at the space beside Hakim.

Hakim moved over, making room for his friend.

"Time to go home, is it?" Maloney spoke again. "Of course, for someone like you or me, home is wherever we happen to be at the moment. Wouldn't you say?" He chuckled under his breath.

A shrill whistle screeched as the train lurched forward along the tracks.

"Tell me, did you ever find the wise one you were looking for?" Maloney's stare was fixed on the moon.

Hakim didn't know how to answer.

"Not to worry. No doubt you have been on quite a journey — a magical one, but aren't they all?"

Maloney smiled as Hakim nodded his head in acknowledgment.

"I'll tell you what we can do to pass the time, my friend," Maloney said with enthusiasm. "Before we reach the city, you can tell me all about your travels, yes?"

Hakim thought for a moment, but didn't know where to begin. Maloney prodded him again. "Well, then, did you find your *self* like I asked you to?" He pulled something from the pocket of his robe. The Universe card. Hakim looked at it, began to understand, and smiled.

"There is only one power that creates everything. I am a part of everyone and everything. The universe is an extension of myself." Hakim waved with his hand at the people surrounding them, speaking softly.

Maloney smiled. "You are absolutely right," he said. "Once you know this, once you truly know who you are, you will never feel alone."

Maloney pulled a card from his hat this time, but Hakim wasn't certain what it was.

"Stillness allows me to hear what my heart is telling me. When I am still, I can listen to my heart and follow my inner wisdom."

Hakim looked down at his lap, where another card of Maloney's had fallen. He turned it over: Chariot.

"I went on a journey to find the secrets of the wise one, but what I learned brought me back to myself. I learned that everyone has a special gift to give to others, and by giving our gift, we fulfill our own dreams." Hakim smiled triumphantly.

The train began to slow as it chugged up a hill, and Hakim leaned back against the pack. Hakim thought about the villagers he had just left. He thought about the fisherman and his love of fishing. Maloney pulled another card from his pocket, but quickly tucked it away. He wanted to hear what Hakim would say without a card to prompt him.

"The path of greatest power is the path of love." Hakim felt confident in his choice of words. Spurred by the surprised look on Maloney's face, he continued.

"Passionate love for life, and compassionate love for everyone and for everything."

"Ah, you have learned the greatest lesson of all," Maloney said quietly.

The train was now rushing through the midnight air. The moon cast a silver glow on everything. Hakim looked at Maloney. His white hair looked almost phosphorescent in the light of the moon.

Hakim thought for a moment. He understood the importance of love and compassion, but he thought of all the terrible things he had seen in the city: the greed, the malice, the evil.

"What about all the terrible things in the world?" He assumed Maloney knew what things he was talking about. "Why are some people so mean and cruel?"

Slowly Maloney began to speak. "This is a crucial piece of the puzzle, Hakim." He lifted his arm and pointed his finger at the woman next to them. "My friend here is a snake charmer. You see the bag?"

Hakim looked down at a brown burlap sack that

lay not two feet from his legs. Sure enough, there was a slow movement inside it.

"The serpent she keeps holds a deadly venom, a poison that could kill you in a moment. That venom, Hakim, is like the greed, envy, and malice within people. There is no way to control whether that snake will bite, and yet there is a way to avoid being bitten.

"When the snake charmer pulls the snake from the bag and makes it dance for her, she knows how to handle it. She understands its nature. The snake will not bite unless it is threatened. People are like that, too, Hakim, except that our actions are less predictable. We all have a deadly venom inside us. We bite when we are afraid and poison others with our thoughts and deeds. It is fear that generates poison; it is fear itself that we must guard against. We cannot control the fear within others, but we can avoid their poison and control our own fearful thoughts."

I control my own choices, and thus control my fate. Lamia's words echoed in Hakim's ears. The sound of Maloney's voice and the rhythmic movement of the train were lulling Hakim into sleep. His eyes kept closing despite his desire to stay awake. He felt Maloney get up and walk away. Hakim opened his eyes in time to see Maloney's white head of hair disappear down the ladder on the side of the train.

Hakim listened to the howling wind rushing by as the train shot through the land. He began to feel the rhythm of the train as the same rhythm of life all around him. For a moment he felt nothing but silent awareness. He was nowhere and everywhere all at once, and suddenly he understood the world for the very first time. There was no past full of sorrow and pain and isolation. There was no future full of promise and hope. There was only the present moment. There was only one power — a glistening light, a liberating energy that flooded and pulsed through everything.

Hakim was soaring. He saw everything, felt everything. He was free and unbounded. He was watching, witnessing the drama of the world unfold all around him. He was writing it, acting in it, directing it. He was the holy man in the corner chanting mantras, and the thief perched at his side. He was the father and the son sitting across from him. He was the snake charmer and the snake, the poison and the healing elixir. He was the mountains shrouded in purple light. He was the moon and the shining stars, the green rice fields and the red desert dust. In that moment, as Hakim lost himself completely, he found out who he really was.

Hakim could not be sure how long he had sat with his eyes closed when he felt a gentle breeze blowing against his cheek. He opened his eyes, and much to his surprise, a woman was sitting across from him.

"Welcome home, child." Her voice was soft and gentle.

Hakim thought to himself that it would be nice if he had a home, but he reasoned that she meant something else.

I must be dreaming, he thought, as he studied her closely. She wore a simple green shawl that draped over her head and fell majestically around her shoulders. Her face was thin and her features fine. She was utterly beautiful. Light radiated from her slender shoulders, illuminating the space around her. Hakim looked down at her hands, expecting to find a green stone planted on a ring around her finger. The woman smiled at Hakim's innocent mistake. When he looked down, he found the ring on his own finger.

Hakim opened his eyes and looked around. The other passengers were quiet and still, some deep in slumber. In front of him a figure began to emerge, climbing up the ladder on the roof. Tall and sleek, it slowly made its way over the bags and sleeping people toward Hakim.

Hakim studied it closely, unafraid. The figure stepped in front of Hakim, concealing the moon and casting a shadow where there had only been white light. The man removed the hood from his head.

Hakim calmly looked up at the Master, as if knowing that he would appear.

"Ah, I have been looking for you, Hakim! I have something important to tell you." The Master was elated that he had found the boy.

"Go away." Hakim spoke softly but firmly.

A peculiar expression crossed the Master's face, making his mustache twitch. He started again, "I have a proposition for you. One that I know you will want to — "

"I will not work for you. Go away." Hakim interrupted him with a confidence that surprised even himself.

The Master smiled, refusing to accept defeat. "Well, perhaps you'd rather starve in the streets, boy, or steal from others for the rest of your life. I'm certain you'll reconsider when you are hungry again. You know where to find me when you do."

The Master stared intently at Hakim. Something about the boy had changed. Somehow, he looked different. *It is something in his eyes.* The Master was adept at reading others; he knew there was nothing he could do to persuade Hakim at the moment. The Master nodded and turned away. Hakim watched his dark figure descend the ladder and disappear into the bowels of the train.

Hakim felt an overwhelming feeling of relief. His heart was beating rapidly, but he was filled with a sense of triumph and joy. Hakim looked down at the card in his lap.

Universe. He put it in his pocket for safekeeping. Just then, the train's whistle pierced the air, as if to express the joy Hakim was feeling. Smoke billowed out of the train's engine and climbed toward the heavens, where the moon could embrace it. The lights of the city twinkled up ahead as the train brought them closer to home.

Hakim smiled with a contentment he had never known before. He had left the city as an orphan, and he was returning as its son.

16

CHILD OF THE DAWN

IT WAS ALMOST DAWN WHEN THE TRAIN SLOWLY
pulled into the main station. It lurched for a
moment, then stopped and blew its whistle to
announce that its destination had been reached. The
train brought instant life to the quiet station as bag-
gage handlers rushed from all sides and loaded heavy
bags onto their heads and shoulders. Passengers
slowly drifted off the train, yawning and stretching
their stiff muscles.

Hakim climbed down and began to make his way to the boarding area. Just then, from the corner of his eye, he spotted Maloney.

"Welcome home." Maloney smiled warmly, his eyes sparkling.

"Thank you," Hakim said.

"Well, my friend, this journey ends, but another one begins."

Hakim thought about all the people he had met. Maloney and all the others would forever be a part of him, in a special place in his heart. Maloney grabbed Hakim and held him in an affectionate embrace. They knew it would not be the last they would see of each other.

Hakim turned and made his way toward the grand gate of the station. It was a beautiful building, a blend of British colonial and Indian architecture. Over the monumental archway hung a clock that read almost half past six. Hakim crossed the threshold of the gate and looked out at the streets. Through the faint light of early dawn, he could see the city come to life like a dance that was perfectly choreographed.

An old man sat next to a bicycle stringing a chain through the spokes of the wheel. The sound of the rattling chain echoed off a stone wall and blended with the morning prayers of a woman kneeling on the balcony above him. The woman stood and moved gracefully — the only sound coming from the thin silver trinkets she wore around her ankles.

Hakim stepped onto the street that emerged from the station gate. A vendor rushed past him toward the station, pushing a cart full of trinkets and souvenirs he would hawk to arriving tourists. Hakim smiled warmly at the man, at the world around him that was once again a part of his life. *Everything looks so different*, he thought. As if altered by the very air around it, the city looked and felt almost new to him. Hakim wondered what it was that had changed. He looked again at the city that surrounded him. Shimmers of light were beginning to dance on the rooftops of the buildings. The streets were quiet except for occasional passing cars. The air was cool and sweet with the fresh scent of morning.

Up ahead, Hakim spotted a solitary figure curled in a corner of a doorstep, shielding itself from the outside world. Hakim drew closer and saw it was a young boy just waking up. He had slept alone on the street, and his clothes were soiled and tattered. The boy sensed Hakim approaching and turned his head to face him.

Hakim crouched down beside the young street orphan.

"Who are you?" the boy asked innocently.

"My name is Hakim." Hakim put his hands behind his neck and unclasped the goldstone necklace that Devi had given him. He took it off and held it in his hands. He thought of the wisdom that Devi had shared with him. *Giving is the instrument through which life sings.*

"This is a necklace a friend of mine gave me. Here, I'd like you to have it." Hakim placed the beaded necklace into the boy's hands.

The boy accepted the gift with a look of surprise and confusion.

"Come on." Hakim reached out and touched the boy on his shoulder. "There is something else I want to share with you. It's a story about a wise one and his secrets to wealth and happiness."

The boy's eyes grew wide with curiosity as he rose and stood beside Hakim.

"You see," — Hakim looked at the boy with a sparkle in his eye — "there was once a wise one who taught me the secret to wealth and happiness. Do you want to know what he said?"

The boy nodded his head and silently stared at Hakim.

Hakim looked into the young boy's eyes. "Everyone has a special gift to give to others. If you listen to the wisdom of your heart, you will know what it is. The secret of happiness is to use your special gift. The secret of wealth is to give your gift to others."

The sun was slowly rising, spreading its warmth upon the land. Rays of golden sunlight burst into the orange and purple sky. The two boys started walking side by side down the dusty road. Hakim stared into the golden rays of light, at the sun that was welcoming him home. Instinctively, he knew there was a promise in store for him. And this promise was like the dawning of a new day.

ALSO FROM AMBER-ALLEN PUBLISHING

The Seven Spiritual Laws of Success by Deepak Chopra

In this classic bestseller, Deepak Chopra distills the essence of his teachings into seven simple, yet powerful principles that can easily be applied to create success in all areas of our lives. (Also available in audio cassette)

Creating Affluence by Deepak Chopra

With clear and simple wisdom, Deepak Chopra explores the full meaning of wealth consciousness and presents simple A-to-Z steps that spontaneously generate wealth in all its forms. (Also available in audio cassette)

The Crescent Moon by Deepak Chopra (Audio Cassette)

This audio celebrates the tender innocence of childhood and the joyous, simple pleasures of living. Deepak Chopra captures the warmth and spirit of Rabindranath Tagore's prose poetry, while sounds of nature and the inspiring flute of G. S. Sachdev grace our listening experience.

Living Without Limits by Deepak Chopra and Wayne Dyer (Audio Cassette)

Two leaders in the field of human potential share their wisdom before a live audience as they question and challenge one another on the importance of quieting the inner dialogue, the power we have to heal ourselves of fatal diseases, the negative impact of the media on our health, and more.

The Legend of Tommy Morris by Anne Kinsman Fisher

From the mystical land of Scotland comes a tale about a man who learned to tap the power of his love to accomplish the seeming impossible. Based on a true story, this book speaks to us about the secrets of universal love, and how we can become a living expression of the spirit and power of love.

Seth Speaks by Jane Roberts

One of the most powerful of Jane Roberts' "Seth Books," this essential guide to conscious living clearly and powerfully articulates the furthest reaches of human potential, and the concept that we all create our own reality.

The Nature of Personal Reality by Jane Roberts

In this perennial bestseller, Seth challenges our assumptions about the nature of reality and stresses the individual's capacity for conscious action.

The Magical Approach by Jane Roberts

Seth reveals the true, magical nature of our deepest levels of being, and explains how we have allowed it to become inhibited by our own beliefs and conventional thinking.

The Oversoul Seven Trilogy by Jane Roberts

One of the most imaginative tales ever written, the adventures of Oversoul Seven are at once an intriguing fantasy, a mind-altering exploration of our inner being, and a vibrant celebration of life.

Amber-Allen Publishing is dedicated to bringing
a message of love and inspiration to all who seek
a higher purpose and meaning in life.

For a catalog of our books and cassettes,
please contact:

AMBER-ALLEN PUBLISHING, INC.
P.O. Box 6657
San Rafael, California 94903-0657